silvan

THE COMPLICATED ROMANTIC LIFE OF ROMY DELACROIX

RIVER CHASTAIN

Cover Design by Sarah M. Cradit at Storyville Designs

Art by Lauren Richelieu

Editing by Jenny Sims at Editing4Indies

Publisher Contact:

Seventh and Pyrtania

riverchastainauthor@gmail.com

the complicated romantic life of romy delacroix

A lycan, a vampire, and a warlock stumble into a witch.

Andromeda Delacroix's uncomplicated life was written in the stars. Marry the man chosen for her by her family. Succeed her mother as high priestess of the Delacroix Coven. Preside over all preternaturals of New Orleans.

Enter Silvan the lycan, Bastian the vampire king, and Dane the sensitive warlock.

Yeaaah… things are about to get complicated.

Silvan

Bastian

Dane

Romy and her men get up to ALL sorts of sexy shenanigans. For a full list of content warnings, please visit www.riverchastain.com

the preternaturals

DELACROIX COVEN (WITCHES)

Location:
Delacroix Manor, New Orleans, Louisiana

High Priestess:
Cassia Delacroix

Notable Members:
Cyril
Romy
Thora
Daphne, former High Priestess
Selene
Loren

Deceased Members:

Alizon

Evadne

Iris

Teche Coven:

Rosemary

Percy

Dane

* * *

RINCEWIND PACK (LYCANS)

Location:

Lycan Woods, outskirts of New Orleans

Pack Leader:

Asa Rincewind

Notable Members:

Silvan

Deceased Members:

Ylfa

* * *

MARCHLAND CLAN (VAMPIRES)

Location:

Le Ville Marchlande, Placquemine Parish, Louisiana

Leader:

Bastian Marchland

Notable Members:

Fenring

Unnamed Vampire

Deceased Members:

Bastian's unnamed brother

To the friendship that brought us here

prologue: the rogue wolf

Silvan Rincewind kept to the perimeter of the clearing. Near enough to be seen and for others to know he was there, but far enough out for others to know he was *watching.*

He already knew what Asa would say before the prideful beast spoke a word. Blah, blah, blah, justice for Claude, their cherished elder and friend, whose drained corpse lay at the center of the clearing, was left to send a message. Everything was according to their laws, which had always been more about politics than justice.

Silvan's hands twitched at his sides. He was ready to shift, to *tear.* He didn't need a fucking pack meeting to tell him a fucking vampire had taken Claude from them. It wasn't even the fang marks on the corpse's neck, though that should have been enough to forego decorum and burn down the Marchand empire until not a single bloody devil remained among them.

No, the vampires had always taken what wasn't theirs. No matter what was said in the forest that night under the harvest moon, Silvan was done watching the vampires carve a trail of blood through their pack.

Wind whipped through the cypress. The stench of the bayou, miles away, was as ripe as though he stood in it up to his knees. He avoided those cursed wetlands whenever he could. The bayou was for the witches, and if Asa dared suggest they summon the coven to deal with pack business...

"Calm yourself before someone gets hurt," Asa said, striding past without so much as a glance his way.

Silvan snarled and reared forward after him. "Someone already *has* gotten hurt, Father. More than hurt. What are we doing here in the forest? What good is talk?" He quickened his stride to keep pace. "We know what we need to do, so let's fucking *do it.*"

Asa spun with such violent fury that Silvan almost forgot the man would never actually hurt him. "Do not tell me how to lead this pack, Sil. Your mother—"

"Is *dead* because of *the same monsters.*" Silvan jutted an arm toward the clearing. He felt the eyes of the rest of the pack on them, quietly reading the feud between father and son. Asa's father would be even angrier about that as he was about any quibble that challenged his authority, but anger about anything other than Claude's killers, who were, at that moment, running around thinking they'd gotten away with it, was a waste of rage. "The vampires have been allowed to roam these forests for too long! Too long they have stalked our elders, our women. One of our children, even—"

"Enough!" Asa boomed. The trees shimmered overhead and to the sides. The pack whispered among themselves. It should have bothered Silvan, but it didn't. He was used to being seen as the rogue wolf, the disappointment. The heir who could never be allowed to become alpha. "You will calm yourself, Silvan Rincewind, or you will go stand with the pack and *not* at my side."

Silvan slammed his mouth shut. Asa had never threatened that before. Sure, he'd always had choice words for his only son, and even Silvan could admit he sometimes deserved them. But Claude had been more than a member of the pack. He'd been family. Asa's late father's brother. One of the very last of the true elders.

Fresh fury whipped through Silvan, and soon he felt the sensation of fur breaking through flesh. Rage-shifting was painful and forbidden, for a wolf shifting through bloodlust was inherently dangerous.

Nose flaring, he grunted and turned away. "No need for threats, Father. I'll stand along the forest line, where I can keep watch. Go on and share your wisdom while Claude rots, unavenged."

Silvan stormed away before his father could rebuke him for the vitriol that was a tad extreme, even for him. He had no intention of apologizing, though, not then nor later, when his blood cooled. If it ever did.

He truly believed he'd never know peace until every last vampire in Louisiana was a pile of ash.

Far from the pack, he could catch wind of any change in scent. He'd feel better if someone else took watch on the other side of the perimeter, but the rest of the pack fed upon Asa's words like they were the only sustenance they'd ever need. They loved the man and worshiped the wolf.

"Beloved brothers and sisters..." Asa stepped up onto the stone dais the pack had dragged into the clearing. Keera, one of the unmatched females, helped him up when he wobbled. He smiled down at her, and she blushed as though they were at a damn cotillion.

She probably hopes Father will pair her with me.

Silvan snorted. Little chance of that happening. The last wolf he wanted to mate with was one who lapped hungrily at the altar of his father's bullshit.

"This is a dark day for the Rincewind Pack," Asa continued. The wind whipped through his long black hair, and for a moment, he resembled a stadium rock god. "And a dark day for me and my kin. Claude was more than one of us. He was my father's brother, my mentor, and my friend. Vengeance is, of course, on all of our minds, but so should be the potential for war."

"Vampires!" someone shouted, and the word caught like wildfire, spreading through the pack in an animated chant.

Silvan smirked and crossed his arms.

Asa listened with godlike patience, and when the chant faded, he held up a hand to silence them. "The fang marks at the neck seem to justify that suspicion." When the pack began to rile and howl, he held his hand higher, and they quieted. "But when vampires have attacked us in the past, they have traditionally left less of a trail. It would almost seem *too* obvious it's a vampire, wouldn't it? As though we were expected to think just that."

Silvan growled, his jaw scissoring in burning agitation. He knew precisely what his father would propose next.

"Thus, we cannot know who our killer is without conducting a full investigation. To do so, we need help from our allies."

"Fucking hell," Silvan hissed. He raked a hand down his stubble and paced.

"But it will not be said that Asa Rincewind made a decision while deep in his own troubled grief. So tonight, we'll put it to a vote. If you believe we should summon the Delacroix Coven to our aid, as is our right, then when I lower my hand again, show me your support by shifting into your true form. If you believe we should handle matters on our own, then stay as you are."

Silvan's gaze flitted across the pack, waiting to see who would give in to his father's weak-ass, pitiful attempt at diplomacy and who would stand and avenge their own, witches be damned.

Asa nodded, surveying the pack with a wistful look before lowering his hand.

The entire forest lit up with fierce howls. The sound of flesh tearing and fangs gnashing drowned out any spoken words.

Asa's solemn face began to smile as he witnessed the unanimous support from the pack.

Had Silvan *really* expected it to go any differently?

Asa could tell them all to leap into the Gulf of Mexico, and nothing would be left of the Rincewind Pack.

"Go, then. *Feast.* Recover your energy. For you will all need it and then some for what lays ahead!"

Silvan watched in stunned rage as the pack leaped into the forest through gaps in the trees, disappearing with whooping, frenzied howls.

When they were gone, Asa turned and fixed his gaze on Silvan.

His mouth twitched in a hard smile, and then he, too, shifted and went to join the pack.

Grudgingly, Silvan did the same, though he had no intentions of hunting that night.

Not *that* kind of hunting anyway.

CHAPTER 1

delacroix royalty

Andromeda Delacroix sank into the plush turquoise pillows on her bed. A few years ago, when she was a junior in high school, turquoise had been her favorite color, but now, in college, she wished for a more sophisticated bed linen. *When you can change it yourself, you may have whatever color scheme you please, Andromeda.* That was Cassia Delacroix's passive-aggressive way of insisting her daughter practice magic more. Romy snapped her fingers and envisioned a deep taupe, but instead of the neutral she'd hoped for, the comforter had turned burnt orange. She frowned and snapped again. Apricot.

A familiar giggle echoed in the hall, and Romy looked up to see her sister peeking around the door.

Thora's fingers clicked together and returned the comforter to its original shade.

Romy scrunched her nose. "You are literally twelve and better than me at magic."

"Nah, I'm just into it more than you." Thora skipped to Romy's side and hopped in bed. After pulling the covers high, she snatched a manila envelope from the bedside table.

"Did you come in here to snoop?"

"Yep." Thora removed the papers from inside. "But it's not snooping if you're my sister. What's yours is mine, and what's mine is yours."

"Remember that the next time we have red velvet cake and I take your portion," Romy quipped with a playful punch to her arm.

Thora's attention was too fixed on her reading material to respond.

"Hello? Red velvet cake... your favorite." Romy waved a hand across her sister's face. "Next time we have it, it's all mine."

"Shut up and let me find out about him. This is so exciting, Ro."

Romy rolled her eyes. "You really were made for this bullshit."

"So were you, even if you don't believe it." Thora cleared her throat. "Dane Teche, son of Rosemary and Percy Teche. Born in White Castle, Louisiana. Graduated Magna Cum Laude from LSU with a double major in political science and psychology, minor in music. Accepted into Tulane School of Law this September."

"Yada, yada, yada." Another eye roll. This one exaggerated for Thora's sake.

"Ohhh, he likes poetry and Homer's *The Iliad*. You like those things too!" Not easily deterred when it came to romantic notions, she pressed the papers to her chest and sighed. "It's a match made in—"

"Hellllll..." Romy cut in.

Thora frowned. With tufts of hair sprouting from her red mane and deep-set dimples, she looked like a toddler ready to burst into a tantrum. It was at those moments when Romy loved her sister most. They fought—and often—but they also shared an unbreakable bond. When their parents had told nine-year-old Romy she would have a sibling before the beginning of autumn solstice, she'd cried and had tried to run away within a week. For the next few months, she refused to speak to anyone. Romy was forced to break her silence, though, when Cassia went into early labor in the middle of a hurricane. With no one else to assist—amid the booming thunder and howling wind—she'd delivered her baby sister. Romy had named her too. Thora, the thunder goddess.

"You're not even going to try?" Thora pleaded.

"Look at him, he's handsome. Looks like one of those hot K-drama actors you think are so sexy."

Romy twisted the photograph to the side and eyeballed it closer. Thora had a point. He wasn't bad looking, and he did seem to have some of the same interests as she did. Maybe he wouldn't be such a bad husband after all.

Since she was old enough to ask her parents how they'd met, Romy had known she, too, would have an arranged marriage. She'd known she was the next leader of the Delacroix Coven even longer. Two extremely heavy burdens for a twenty-one-year-old to carry, and she didn't want either responsibility.

For all the ways Romy complied with her mother and the coven, a piece of her was dying to break free, longing to be more than what was expected.

But for the unforeseeable future... conformity was her only choice.

"Of course I'm going to try. I don't want Mom blowing a gasket. She still hasn't recovered from your little stunt with the cinnamon rolls."

"What can I say? I like cream cheese icing. It's not my fault if I read Mom's recipe wrong. Her handwriting is so messy." Thora's laughter resonated above them, and immediately, her hands went over her mouth.

"Shhh," Romy chastised. "You know it's way past your bedtime."

"I'm almost a teenager. I should get to stay up past ten thirty."

Romy clicked her tongue. "Take it up with the boss. I had a ten thirty bedtime until I graduated from high school. Those are the breaks for being *Delacroix royalty.*" She said the last words with exaggerated air quotes.

"Yeah, no joke," Thora agreed, her voice an octave lower. "So why was Dane the one chosen for you? What makes him unique? Besides his intellectually good looks?"

The answer wasn't complicated. Something about *bloodlines* and the *great and auspicious history of the Delacroix Coven*. But it was more than Romy wanted to delve into tonight, especially with her eager sister who—in Romy's opinion—was a million times better suited to carry on the family name than she could ever hope to be. "A bunch of crap. The coven's breeding program is an exact art. We're just the cattle."

"Better not let your mother hear you talk like that, my little sunrise," a deep voice said from the hallway. Their father, Cyril Delacroix, stepped inside Romy's room and sat on the edge of the bed. Thora leaped over the pillows and into his lap when he opened his arms.

Romy smiled at the pet name he'd given her when she was born. *My Andromeda is perfect, like the dawn. She's my own little sunrise.* The sisters shared a closer relationship with their dad than they did with their mom. Partly because Cassia's duties often pulled her from their family but mostly because of Cyril's gentle and nurturing demeanor. Their family called him *Father Earth* as an inside joke, a nod to his Element and kind-hearted personality. He had been the one to kiss their skinned knees and tell them bedtime stories, and during school programs, they looked for Cyril's face in the crowd.

Romy surmised her mom wasn't jealous of the bond. In fact, she seemed grateful. Not only was Cassia the high priestess of the largest coven in Louisiana but she also presided over the High Council of Preternaturals, a demanding and exhausting job that required accountability and confidence in equal measure. All the more reason for Romy to abdicate—or whatever it was next-in-line high priestesses did.

"Hi, Daddy." Thora kissed his cheek. "We were just talking about Romy's new *boyfriend*, Dane."

Romy's good humor faded. "He's not my boyfriend, Thora."

"*Yet*." She punctuated the word with a head nod. "Not *yet*. Hey, Dad, why was Dane chosen to be Romy's mate? I think she knows but just doesn't want to tell me."

Cyril tapped his wrist, pretending it was a watch. "I'll tell you, but then you've got to get to bed. Not enough sleep makes grumpy witches. Romy should know. She hates sleeping."

"Maybe you *need* to take some naps, sis, for your candescence to happen." Thora grinned at her simple solution.

"Maybe so." If only it was that easy for Romy to activate her powers, she would have taken all the naps in the world. No one had hassled her about her lack of skill as a witch, least of all Cyril and Thora. They'd been overly encouraging and supportive with Cyril coaching her every free minute available. Even her mom had reassured her that some of the most masterful conjurers were late bloomers.

But Romy couldn't help holding herself to a higher standard. A witch had to be able to do more than change the color of a bedspread. A coven leader had to be able to do so much more. "So, Dad, tell this little monster what's so great about Dane Teche."

Before Cyril could answer, Thora's hand went to her chest, and she coughed.

"You okay, sweetheart?" he asked.

"Yes, sir," she said quietly. "Just a catch in my throat. Tell us, please."

"You two already know the reasons covens are female-led, I assume."

"Our capabilities infinitely exceed our male counterparts!" Thora beamed as she recited from one of their sacred texts. Her smile dissolved as a dark thought passed over her eyes. "One day, I'm really going to be more powerful than you?"

Cyril agreed with a nod. "You already are, angel. Like Romy, you're just waiting for candescence. Dane's mother, Rosemary is a descendant of the prestigious Teche Coven from Romania and has shown exemplary healing capabilities throughout her life. Then there's Dane's father, Percy, he's a master at controlling his Fire Element. Any of their sons will make a suitable match for Romy, and that strengthens our bloodline. Our lineage is as much about preservation as it is procreation."

"But aren't we all, like, related somehow?" Thora made a sour face.

"Distantly, yes, but most of those branches go way back."

"Did you love Mom when you were sealed to her?" Romy surprised herself with her inquiry. She'd never questioned much about coven marriages because details gave her future as the high priestess validity. For years, she'd subscribed to the belief that disinterest would cause the cup to pass from her hands to another more suitable member, but there she was with a chosen mate and an appointment with an all-to-soon destiny.

Cyril swallowed hard as if he didn't want to offer the

truth. "No, I didn't love her at the time. Not at all. I *tolerated* Cassia as she did me."

"But you love her *now*, don't you?" Thora said, urgency in her voice. Clearly, she didn't like the idea of contention between her parents. Romy didn't either.

"With all that I am, Thora. With everything in me."

Romy did some quick addition and subtraction in her head. Her parents were married fifteen years before she was born. "You didn't love each other until you had me, did you?"

"After we married, I grew to love her as one loves a friend or a relative. But you're right. I didn't fall in love with her until we got pregnant with you, Romy. I hope and pray to The One and The Only that it doesn't take you and Dane so many years to fall in love, but if loving him doesn't come naturally, know that it will come. Good things always come to those who wait."

Before Romy could ask any follow-up questions, Cyril squinted at the bedside clock. "Mom would skin me alive if she knew you were still up, Miss Priss. How 'bout a drink of water for your throat before I tuck you in?"

Using deep concentration, Thora closed her eyes and inhaled. A glass levitated from the dresser, then settled into her hands. After a big grin, she skipped to her room, and her father followed.

Romy glanced again at the picture of Dane and sighed.

SEVERAL MINUTES LATER, CYRIL RETURNED TO Romy's door. "May I come in again?"

"Sure." Romy patted the place where he'd sat earlier. "She's good, Dad. Thora. She's... gifted."

"Yes, she is. A quick study and an eager learner. But don't be disheartened. Your time will come, and it will be perfect for you."

"What if my powers never activate and all my kids are duds because I suck at being a witch? Then I get to add invalidating the entire Delacroix Dynasty to my list of failures."

Cyril's head shook from side to side. "Impossible. This *will* happen. You just need to be patient and have some faith in yourself. I believe in you. So does Thora." He cupped her chin to look directly in her eyes. "And contrary to what you may believe, your mother does too."

"Hmph. I'm not so sure. Maybe she believes in my ability to be a smart-ass about the things I don't agree with her on, but I don't think she's too confident I'll excel at witchcraft."

"Well, I have proof otherwise. It's the original reason I came upstairs to see you tonight. An emergency convergence of the High Council has been requested, and Mom wants you there."

She raised an eyebrow. To be invited to sit in with the High Council without activated powers was an enormous honor. Composed of the most elite preternaturals, their meetings were held at the witching hour every full moon at one of their most sacred places—*Tuiteam feòil is fuil.*

While Romy had little interest in how witches handled their personal business, the lives of different preternaturals had always fascinated her. Other than the random faerie or elf stopping by Delacroix Manor to speak about council business, Romy's exposure to other magical beings had been limited to field trips to the Preternatural Constabularies Headquarters. Cassia and Cyril weren't prejudiced; they simply followed the long-held rule of little-to-no fraternization between the races.

Romy thought it was a stupid rule, and when the time was right, she would question her mother about it.

"Seriously? She wants me to come to the High Council?"

"Yeah, seriously. Take a look for yourself." Cyril removed his phone from his pocket, punched some buttons, and passed it to Romy.

Romy read the text messages between her parents at least three times, and the words didn't change.

. . .

Cassia: pot roast in the crock pot for tonight's supper. Sorry I won't be home. Problems with Asa and the RW pack again

Cyril: Not surprised. He's not been the same since Ylfa died. We'll save you a plate in the fridge.

Cassia: You're right. He's just requested a meeting with the High Council. Don't want to do it, but in the name of keeping the peace...

Cassia: What do you think about Andromeda attending? I think it's time.

Cyril: It would be a good experience for her. She'd prob be more interested in coven business if she saw what you did firsthand.

Cassia: Ask her for me, if you will. And call a sitter for Thora.

"Well..." Cyril leaned in. "Do you want to go?"

A smile tugged at the corners of Romy's mouth. Yes, she absolutely one hundred percent did want to go. "I can be ready in fifteen minutes."

CHAPTER 2

between the lycan and the vampire

Despite being the end of July, a bitter wind sent a chill up Romy's spine as she followed her parents through the marsh to *Tuiteam feòil is fuil*. Louisiana's weather was hardly ever frigid. Even in winter, temperatures usually persisted in the high thirties or forties, and "blistering hot" wasn't an accurate description of their torturous summers. But tonight, Romy could have sworn she felt ice crunch beneath her feet. She glanced ahead at her mother's silhouette, certain she'd see frozen crystals falling from the water witch's fingers, but nothing was there.

Was it the mystical surroundings, or Romy's overactive imagination?

The land was unlike any other place she'd ever visited. An ancient darkness spread across the earth as a dense fog obscured the ground. Romy sensed the tortured souls who roamed in and out of the marshland. More, she heard their whispers. Though foreboding, they would not harm anyone—at least no one who still breathed. The ghostly dead operated by a different, more malevolent code than the living. These Shadow Wraiths resulted from the Hundred Years War—a bloody struggle for territory and domination primarily between vampires and lycans. Inevitably, all preternaturals were caught in the madness and suffered.

The clash lasted from the founding of New Orleans in 1718 until 1818, when Romy's fourth great-grandmother and the Delacroix Coven intervened. Following several failed attempts at diplomatic resolution, Alizon Delacroix realized the pride of both races would keep them from seeking peace, so the coven used whatever means possible to subdue the conflict. Employing black magic was their last resort, but when faced with the extinction of their kind, it was an absolutely necessary decision.

To maintain control and exert domination, Alizon and her coven drained the stagnant black blood of the vampires, then burned the bodies of the lycans into ashes. After combining the two—for one hundred days and one hundred nights—the coven forced the remainder of the opposing sides to consume the mixture, a reminder to never attempt supremacy over the other again. The Delacroix Coven became the self-appointed mediators and their high priestess, the mouthpiece of The One and The Only and leader of the High Council, presiding over all preternaturals.

Their pace quickened. The deeper they went into the wetlands, the thicker the fog became. Unable to see her father's cloak any longer, Romy followed the sound of his shuffling until the howls and other bizarre sounds inside *Tuiteam feòil is fuil* became too loud for her to hear anything else. The fires burning ahead guided her the rest of the way.

As Romy came closer to the derelict ruins, she determined it wasn't several fires but one large blaze encapsulating the entire area. Stone columns covered in velvety green moss and wisteria vines soared overhead to create a canopy filled with every different kind of flower, but primarily crimson gerbera daisies. Romy grinned at the sight of her mother's favorite flower. Clearly, Cassia had a hand in the decoration.

An even, steady drumbeat heralded the arrival of the high priestess and the entire Delacroix family as the inferno parted down the middle to allow them passage. Though determined to keep her attention on Cyril's head while they marched inside, Romy couldn't help but gawk at the distinctive clusters of preternaturals. The fae were petite, wispy creatures, some with wings, some without, and all with light hair. The elves were easily over six feet tall, with long hair, pointed ears, and stoic faces. Dwarves were short and stout, and centaurs were lean and muscled. Each group appeared to have no more than three to seven representatives, except for one. Romy didn't see any defining magical features, but she knew who they were simply by their large number and loudness.

Clad entirely in denim and leather, the lycans of the Rincewind Pack resumed their rowdy banter as soon as Cassia took her seat. In Romy's peripheral vision, she captured the gaze of a man who shouldn't have stood out among his peers, but he did. Like them, he was raucous and unruly, with a woman on each arm, but when they locked eyes, Romy felt something she'd never felt before: desire.

This man *knew* her. He knew her skin, her body. He knew she liked to be kissed hard and how she wanted to be held down with her arms over her head. He knew the way she rolled a nipple between her thumb and forefinger right before she came, and he knew she liked to masturbate in public and nearly get caught.

And...

He knew she was a virgin, and this turned him on the most.

Romy shivered. She tried to avert her eyes, but his glare had locked on her, laser-focused on every move. Entranced, she watched him lash his tongue to lick the air. Back and forth. Slowly. As if he was between her legs, tasting the arousal he'd caused. This man knew she was wet. And he wanted her. *Now.*

A jolt of pleasure went to her core and triggered an ache. She'd been turned on many times but never so thoroughly.

"Romy?" Cyril pointed toward her cousin. "Take a seat next to Loren."

She couldn't respond. All she could think about was the bulge straining against the lycan's jeans and what it would feel like to be beneath him.

"*Romy*," he repeated, tone sharp. "Take your place; you're stalling the line."

"Oh, sorry. Crap." Romy looked over her shoulder to see other coven members waiting behind her, then saw her mother's scowl. She quickly sat next to her cousin.

"Pretty crazy sight, huh, cuz?" Loren said. The daughter of Cassia's sister, Loren was several years older than Romy. She'd manifested her candescence early and had been attending High Council for over a decade.

"What?" Romy leaned closer, barely able to hear above the noisy wolf pack.

"I said this is crazy."

Above them, their grandmother patted both their shoulders. "Two of my three favorite granddaughters. Welcome to the madness, dear Romy."

Romy looked behind her to see their matriarch and former High Priestess Daphne Delacroix along with row after row of other esteemed relatives. As the supreme preternaturals, her family had more members present, and their vote carried more weight. The fact that Romy was there—especially without activated powers—was an honor and something she'd be mindful of going forward.

No more fantasies about forbidden lycan men.

Romy hoped conversation with her cousin and grandmother would help her lose interest in the Rincewind Pack, but their raucousness made it nearly impossible for anyone to focus on anything *but* them. A few of the men spewed beer across the crowd and several groups of three or four wrestled on the ground. But not her lycan. His concentration was resolute. A woman nibbled at his neck, and another sucked his earlobe, but his interest focused on one place and one place only.

Romy.

She swallowed a lump in her throat.

"Oh, wow! This is getting *wild*." Loren's hand covered her mouth. "The pack is going insane."

"Yeah, it's like nothing I've ever seen before." Literally. He was like nothing Romy had ever seen. Who the hell *was* he? And how the fuck had he gotten under her skin so easily? This meeting was the biggest moment in Romy's life, and all she could do was lust after a man she'd never met from a race she was forbidden from associating with.

"My daughter will bring us to order soon enough," Daphne reassured.

Romy's head snapped back and forth and refocused on the center of the ruins and her mother's response to the pack's disorderly conduct. Cassia had never been one to overreact or raise her voice to get her point across. She preferred quieter methods of management.

On cue, Cassia pursed her lips and a frigid blast of ice shot from her fingers, landing on the offending members. Each one of them froze mid-action, including the two girls draped on the lycan's arms. After a shrug, he twisted to remove himself from their grasp and sauntered over to an older man with long black hair. Flanking their sides were two men and three women who looked so similar they could be closely related.

"Asa, you know the rules about numbers." Cassia's timbre remained even. "Three to seven. That is all."

He bowed. "Yes, ma'am."

The pack snarled, minus the frozen and the six next to Asa.

"You heard her. Move," Asa bellowed. "*Now.*"

Chunks of ice fell from bodies, and as the stationary members came back to life, a hole opened in the fiery paramcter for them to exit. When they were gone, only the seven remained.

"My apologies, High Priestess." He took another bow. "Thank you for agreeing to meet with us on such short notice. The pack has suffered a great loss tonight, and we demand justice. Earlier in the—"

"Asa." Cassia interrupted. "You also know the rules about *all* preternatural representatives being present." She pointed to her right and an empty spot. "I cannot hear your complaint without Monsieur Marchland."

He dug his heels into the boggy ground and kicked up a clod of dirt. "The cause of every last one of my damn problems."

"Because they fucking killed Claude!" Romy's lycan exclaimed.

"Son," Asa sighed, frustrated. "Take a step back."

The lycan's face reddened, and he seemed to grow half a foot. "Why should I? Why'd we even come here? We should've found the cunts ourselves and wasted their black blood for the world to see."

"Silvan," Cassia said calmly. She turned to Asa. "One more outburst from your son, and I'll hold him in contempt of my authority. Regulate him, or I will."

Silvan.

Silvan.

That was Romy's lycan's name. Silvan. In her studies of Roman mythology, she recalled the name meant *man of the woods*. How fitting for the son of a pack leader.

"Yes, ma'am. Absolutely. He's upset." Asa patted Silvan's back. "Sil, come on. I know it's hard, but Uncle Claude wouldn't want it this way."

"You know what Claude would want, Father? To live. That's what the motherfucker would want." Silvan wiped his face with the back of his hand. "That's what Claude would want."

"I know. I know he would."

Unable to be consoled, Silvan stormed off behind his family. Romy observed her mother's grimace in obvious disapproval, but Cassia remained quiet. Clearly, the Rincewind Pack was distressed about a deceased member named Claude. Vampires—or the lack thereof at High Council—were another thing upsetting the pack. Despite the truce and the rules both sides abided by, Romy deduced there was no love lost between vampires and lycans. In fact, they still seemed downright hostile.

"Who exactly are we waiting on again?" Romy whispered to Loren.

"Bastian. Bastian Marchland. He's kinda the vampire king of New Orleans," Loren gushed.

"*Vampire king*?" Romy didn't remember hearing anything about any sovereigns other than Cassia's position as head of the High Council. "Really?"

"No, not really. But he's the oldest vamp in town. Mom said he's been around since before the Hundred

Years War, but I'm not sure. Nobody knows much about him, and I think he likes it that way."

Mysteries intrigued Romy. Hell, vampires and lycans and other preternaturals intrigued her, and this only amplified the intrigue. "Is he always this late?"

"Mm-hmm."

The fire dimmed until it was nearly pitch black, and the thick fog outside *Tuiteam feòil is fuil* seeped in. Asa's cigarette fell from the corner of his lips, and his family gathered in a circle and crouched. Were they protecting him?

Whether consciously or unconsciously, every preternatural took a joint step back except for Cassia, who rose from her seat and moved to the center of the ruins.

As quick as Romy could blink, a man dressed in a dark-brown frock coat glided past them. *Bastian*. In all her twenty-one years, Romy had never read the emotions of someone so obviously, so glaringly. His pain, his joy, his fears, and insecurities—she absorbed each one as if they were her own. Though she'd been told vampires had no heart, Romy saw that too. His heart. Could all witches see vampires in this way?

Bastian stopped in front of Cassia and bent at the waist. She acknowledged his respect with a reverent nod. Already, Romy noticed the creature was different from anyone she'd ever seen. But there was something else, something more to him that Romy couldn't identify. It was familiar and peaceful.

A young fae woman with long blond locks fluttered beside Bastian and landed directly to his left. "High Priestess, it is an honor to be here with you this evening. I apologize for my tardiness."

Had the faerie just spoken to Romy's mom as Bastian?

Weird.

"Thank you, Monsieur Marchland. It's no problem, really."

"Hell yes, it is." One of the younger lycan males spoke up. A brother or cousin to Silvan, perhaps. "The vamp's always fucking late. Don't guess he has to follow the same ru—"

"*Silence*," Cassia hissed. Frigid water droplets peppered the arena. "This is my domain, and my judgment is law."

Romy watched Asa attempt to keep his family quiet. He seemed to be diplomatic, a quality she admired. Silvan, on the other hand, hummed with rage.

"High Priestess. Forgive us. We'll remain quiet throughout the remainder of our time here." Asa leveled a glare on the pack. "Won't we?"

"Yeah, yeah," came the chorus of wolf men. Silvan lingered in their shadows with an ever-growing scowl.

“Thank you, Asa. And, Bastian, thank you for coming. Please take your place so we can get started.”

Romy tilted her head toward Loren. “What’s with the faerie chick?”

“Oh, Bastian cannot, under any circumstances, speak to a witch. It’s a part of his *mystery*.”

What an odd rule. Romy wondered who had mandated that vampires couldn’t speak to witches? And why? “Yeah, totally.”

“Thank you all for gathering tonight in our nine-hundred-seventy-fifth convening of the Witches’ High Council. I, Cassiopeia Delacroix, call this convocation to order. We honor the fallen with peace…”

She paused and waited for the assembly to all stand and join in. “With justice. With truth and our commitment to never allow history to repeat itself. By Blood and Flesh, we were divided. By Blood and Flesh, we are also joined.”

“Thank you. You may take your seats. Asa Rincewind, the High Council will hear your complaint.”

With as much hostility as he’d had earlier, Asa stormed to the center of the ruins. “It’s like this, ma’am. My uncle isn’t here with us, his beloved family, because we found him dead last night. The great Claude Rincewind was murdered. *Murdered*. On his own land, where he’d run since he was a pup, near his children and all his grands and great-grands. We've come for *justice.*"

"Yeah, justice," the pack echoed, except Silvan, who was quiet, arms folded across his chest.

"I'm truly so sorry for the loss of Claude. I have years of fond memories of him participating in our council." Cassia's face relaxed. "He was a noble lycan. Let us take a moment to remember him now."

The congregation followed her direction and closed their eyes.

"Such a terrible loss..." Cassia continued after several moments. "But murder is a formidable crime, Asa. What evidence have you compiled?"

"Claude had puncture wounds to his neck." Asa's hands encircled his throat, then he pointed at the center of his chest. "No blood. No heart. I've never in my years come across any other criminal who leaves such a signature."

"None except fucking vamps," Silvan growled despite his father's frown. "What? If you won't say it, I will."

A collective gasp sounded, and after a few seconds, it happened again.

"Asa Rincewind, the penalty for slander is death by the hooves of a centaur. Does your son want to recant his statement?"

Silvan twitched his nose, glaring.

"Of course he does," Asa said reasonably, the warning flashing in his eyes as he leveled a hard gaze on Silvan. "Right, Son?"

"*Do you want to recant your statement*?" she asked again, louder.

"Fuck if I'm recanting anything," he spat. "Not a damn word of it."

Several in the pack sounded a supportive howl.

Asa hung his head with a protracted sigh. "High Priestess, what we want is an investigation. A fair one, which is our right under our laws. That is all we ask."

Cassia's teeth clamped inside her lip, then she glanced at Cyril. To most, this action would appear normal—a wife seeking the support of her husband—but Romy knew better.

Her mother was frightened.

Apprehension had no place in Cassia's world. Romy couldn't recall her mother ever being scared about anything. Not when she'd rid the entire Southern United States of a goblin infestation. Not when she'd turned a hurricane away from New Orleans. Not even when she'd fought the incubus who nearly kidnapped her daughters.

But now? Cassia was genuinely afraid, yet no one—sans her husband and daughter—would ever know. Fear was weakness, and weakness was not allowed.

"If this is your choice, present your testimony, and

we will begin an investigation into this matter immediately."

Asa attempted to make eye contact with Bastian, but Bastian would not engage him or anyone. "It's come to my attention that new vamps are in town. Not one, but two."

Cassia drew back.

"I assumed you didn't know, ma'am. As far as I can tell, they haven't registered with the PC yet."

"No, no new entries have been added in the Preternatural Constabularies in over a month," Cassia confirmed.

"Fucking shocker, that," Silvan quipped.

Asa flinched but didn't directly address Silvan's growing insubordination. "The question is... did *Monsieur Marchland* know they were in his territory... detective that he is."

"I'll ask the questions, Asa. Too easily, you forget your place and the breadth of these charges. I will not speak to you any longer." Cassia pointed a finger at his mouth, and an imaginary needle sewed his top lip to his bottom. "Silvan Rincewind, please continue on your father's behalf. But *watch* your tone with me, for I am in no mood to suffer crazed fools this evening."

"Mmm... mmm," Asa squealed as he tried to pry open the invisible stitches.

"Keep struggling, and I'll make it permanent."

Silvan screwed his mouth together in a tight frown. His nostrils flared as he sucked in the cold night air, bracing. "High Priestess, we would appreciate any assistance in the discovery of who killed Uncle Claude." He grumbled a low roar, burying it with a hard look at the sky. "Please."

"I shall take your petition under consideration." Cassia scribbled something on a paper and passed it to her sister, Selene. "Monsieur Marchland, will you please approach?"

Bastian and his interpreter were in front of Cassia before she set down her pen.

"Did you know new vampires were in New Orleans?"

"Yes, ma'am," the faerie said. She didn't appear to be in a trance, nor did she need to have physical contact with Bastian to assist him, which made Romy wonder if he could read and control minds.

If so, could he read hers?

"And did you evaluate them properly before allowing them to settle?"

"Yes, ma'am."

"Did you report their arrival to the PC?" Her hushed voice was still audible.

Bastian shook his head.

"No, ma'am. This is my mistake," said the faerie. "We've had other distractions, and we'll rectify this immediately. But I am certain they were not involved in the death of Claude Rincewind."

Cassia tilted her head ever so slightly. "How so?"

"I can provide an alibi."

She exhaled, relieved. "You can?"

"I can. If you will send an agent to *Le Ville Marchlande* tomorrow, I can offer video footage of their whereabouts for the past several evenings."

"Bullshit," Silvan spat.

"That's fucking ridiculous!" another lycan called out. "We want justice!"

Unsatisfied with Bastian's answer, the three women and two men shifted into wolf form. Romy's pupils widened to take it all in. In one fluid motion, their bodies split at the head and peeled down the middle like a snake, leaving behind a powdery skin-like residue. Five wolves snarled, then threw back their heads to howl into the night sky. Silvan didn't shift but extended his neck and joined in a howl, defiant and proud. Asa's eyes widened as he looked around his pack in stunned disbelief. It was obvious he disagreed with their impulsiveness.

Outside *Tuiteam feòil is fuil*, the pack responded to their call, an eerie, haunting howl that she would've given her shivers if she'd been alone in the woods. One of the wolves nudged Asa's hand and whimpered as if to say come with us, but Asa jerked from his reach, then turned his back. The shifted wolves vaulted over the fire and into the darkness, but Silvan hung back and paced near his father.

Asa's hands folded over his belly, and he offered an apologetic look in Cassia's direction. The stitches across his mouth disappeared. "High Priestess, I apologize for our behavior. We are all, naturally, grieving a great loss. Claude's death cannot possibly be mistaken for an accident. Yes, new vampires are in town, and yes, we hope you will consider this when you conduct your investigation."

"Thank you, Asa." Cassia offered a closed-mouth smile, one of regret and sadness. "But you know this doesn't exempt your son from his accusation or the penalty that comes with it should it be proven false? Our peace is fragile, and any threat to it—"

"Must be eliminated," he finished. "Yes, ma'am, I know."

"I'll send a team to the Lycan Woods first thing tomorrow morning. Certainly, I know you'll want to perform Claude's last rites as soon as possible. Again, we are so sorry for this loss."

"Thank you, High Priestess."

She nodded, then with a lift of her hand, she dismissed him and the council. The fiery circle vanished, and torches lit up the area in their place, revealing a massive banquet table filled with various food and beverages. Each group dispersed to socialize with the others.

"High Council is the only occasion when we're able to mix with other preternaturals." With a flick of her wrist, Loren materialized two golden goblets and offered one to Romy. "We'll celebrate with wine. And it's not just any wine, either. It's a special fae blend, and if you can drink more than one glass, I'll give you a hundred bucks." She disappeared into the crowd.

Though Romy was interested in the wine, the food, and socialization among races, the lycan's whereabouts fascinated her more. *Her* lycan. *Silvan*. Was he still there? She rose to her tiptoes and strained to see above everyone until she saw his mess of dark curls near the exit.

As if he knew she was thinking about him, he pivoted on his left foot, and they locked eyes again. This time, he winked. The action wasn't blatantly sexy, but she felt a burn between her legs just the same. No way in hell would she make it all the way back to New Orleans without relief. Maybe there would be a moment for her to slip away unnoticed?

WITH SILVAN GONE, ROMY TURNED HER attention to Bastian and his ongoing discussion with Cassia—or rather, the fae's discussion. Unable to get closer, she focused on her mother, on the point of her nose and the kelly green of her eyes. Then she imagined Bastian, but instead of physical features, she envisioned *more*. She'd hoped to hear actual words exchanged, but what she saw was far superior: his soul. His kindness, his hatred of being misunderstood, his love for simple things like wildflowers growing in a field or hummingbirds fluttering around in the springtime. His sorrow, so deep it threatened to consume everything.

Then...

Bastian saw *her*.

Her insecurities about her lack of magical abilities. The fear of disappointing her mother. Her deep and abiding love for Thora. The peace she found beneath the moon.

Andromeda, you are mine.

Laid bare, Romy looked away.

Between the lycan and the vampire, she was spent. She couldn't stay in this place any longer.

Down by the river, Romy slid her hand between her legs. Her thoughts tossed in and out like the waves, gravitating between the two men she'd encountered tonight. Two *different* men. Not once but twice, Romy's walls had been breached.

With Silvan, it was primal. A sensual lust. A carnal feast.

And with Bastian... a different kind of nakedness. Romy was defenseless. Unprotected. Exposed.

Both men pervaded her senses, and she reached the summit of pain and bliss.

To her left, amber eyes shined so brightly that she could see their reflection in the water.

To her right, a figure stood tall, concealed in the shadows. Both watching. Both waiting.

Both wanting.

With that thought, Romy surrendered to the pleasure and cried out into the night.

CHAPTER 3

that witch

Silvan gave the blonde's ass an encouraging squeeze, and it was all she needed to hasten her stride. Her tits moved in almost annoyingly perfect circles like she'd practiced the motion to impress men. He *was* impressed but not enough to remember her name, which was either Flora or Fauna or… fuck, it was probably neither, but if he didn't stop thinking about her fucking stupid name and inconceivably gyrating mammaries, he would never come.

And he needed to come so he could kick the albeit perfectly pleasing ladies out of his room and *think.*

Red hair lashed him in the face. He spat to expel it from his mouth, startling the blonde, whose tits settled down with her slowing stride.

"What's wrong, love? Doesn't it feel good?"

Silvan slapped her ass and grunted through his frustration, losing his focus... losing the climb to the climax he needed.

The hair had been in his imagination, and he knew who it belonged to, and it was fucking unacceptable.

Un. Acc. Cept. A. Ble.

There was no reason a *witch* should be tickling his libido. Even attending a High Council meeting made him need a shower. The highbrow bitches who had no respect for men, for anyone, really, because at their core, they believed they were at the helm of the council because they were better than all the other races. Only a few remained who hadn't forgotten exactly how the witches came to and kept their undeserved power.

"Fine," he growled. His mouth and jaw barely moved. Fucking witch. "Just like that."

The blonde, unlikely named either Flora or Fauna, returned to her fevered rocking, but now she glared at him like he was insane. Well, he probably was because he could still feel that witch's hair on his lips, and even worse, he wanted to devour it, devour *her.*

"You're so hard, daddy." The blonde lied because he wasn't hard, not at all, and he was never, ever going to come like this. He could still taste her on his mouth—he might walk away satisfied from this ill-fated tryst, but she sure hadn't—and suddenly, he saw the witch's slit parting, glistening for *him,* and then he was hard as a fucking boulder.

No. No, fucking no, no, no, no, no. He grunted and forced the witch from his mind.

Andromeda. That was her name. Andromeda Delacroix. But they'd called her something else.

"Are you sure you're up for this...?" The blonde slowed again.

"Romy." He growled the name hard enough to rumble the bed, causing the other two women who were glued to their phones to look up.

"Who's *Romy*?" the blonde asked. She stopped altogether, and he knew then that even if she shoved his cock straight down her esophagus, he would never come for her.

"Her name is Farren," the redhead said, rolling her eyes at the other girl. "Never were good with names, though, were you, wolf?"

"You." He harnessed the raw fury rippling through him, clenching through the most gentle lifting he could manage, and set the blonde aside as easily as a doll. She pouted through every second before bouncing off the bed. Her high, pert ass was nearly perfect, and on any other day...

Fucking Andromeda Delacroix.

Yes, that's what I'd like to be doing right now.

Silvan ran his tongue over his lips and waggled his

fingers at the redhead whose name he *also* couldn't remember. "You."

"Again?" She laughed and stood, stretching her long, lithe frame. She didn't look like the witch, not really, only the hair was similar, but she'd do.

He pulled her up onto the bed, flipped her over, and slid into her still-wet pussy with only seconds to spare before he exploded. Finally.

"Should I take that as a compliment or an insult?" she asked. Still on all fours, she looked over her shoulder with both brows raised.

"Take it however you want," he panted and rolled onto his back. Romy's wide eyes haunted his soul. He felt the pinch of her shoulder blades as he lathed his tongue between them on his way down to—

"Sil?"

"That's all for tonight, ladies," he managed to get out before falling into a dead sleep.

It was past midnight when he woke up. The distant and near calls of the pack hadn't been what stirred him, though *those* were another reminder of what he should be doing—ripping, tearing, feasting in mourning for a man he had loved more than his own father.

No, another nightmare had roused him.

Why he still dreamed of her when it had been years since he'd been a pup, ripped from her arms, was a mystery, and trying to solve it had brought him nothing but more unwelcome pain.

Still as naked as he'd been when the three women left, Silvan rolled out of bed and planted his feet on the cold floor. The jolt snapped him awake. He stretched to bring himself the rest of the way there.

Silvan rolled his shoulders, and a series of satisfying cracks followed. He pulled the curtain aside just a bit and saw the woods brimming with life. Once again, he was reminded he should be there with his people. His pack. The pack that, unless he died first, he would one day lead as the alpha.

High Council had been a fucking joke, resulting in a pointless investigation of pure theater. Everyone knew it had been a vamp. Even Bastian, the weird, broody leader of the pale freaks. Oddly, he seemed concerned, but all that probably meant was that he now had an inconvenient problem to deal with.

He hadn't missed the fucker eyeing Andromeda, either. Rumor was, the vamp couldn't even get it up anymore and cried before feeding. But he'd gotten it up, all right, and that stingy bitch Cassia had noted it, too.

Romy.

"What would you say to me if you were still here, Mom?" Silvan dragged his hands down his face, tugging at his jaw with an extra scrape. "You'd tell me I was fucking insane, wouldn't you?" He cringed and whipped his head. "Sorry, Ma. I know how you dislike it when I cuss. Nah, you'd tell me to shift and go show the pack I'm with them on this. But I'm not, am I? If Father wants to play nice with the witches, that's on him. And if the pack wants to follow? Can't stop 'em."

Silvan pictured Bastian's hungered gaze, fixed on Romy.

"That dead man," he growled, just as his skin began to split and change, "is gonna be a dead man for real. And I can't wait to be the last thing he ever sees."

CHAPTER 4

pertinent questions

Romy had spent most of the morning telling Thora about her night—minus the time by the river, of course. Her sister had listened with her mouth gaped open for over an hour, then had asked a million questions that Romy didn't have answers for.

Hopefully, this was about to change.

Cassia had texted after breakfast and asked Romy to meet in her office, presumably to converse about all she'd seen and heard during High Council. Given the unforeseen events, Romy wasn't surprised. Her mother had always taken the time to explain the inner workings of magic carefully so her daughters would maintain a healthy respect and continue their traditions with the same reverence as their ancestors.

Cassia's psychology practice was at the corner of Natchez and Tchoupitoulas in the Central Business District. The drive from Napoleon Avenue and Delacroix Manor should have taken around half an hour with traffic, but Romy made it in fifteen without magic. *With* magic, she could do it in five, but she usually ended up closer to Mother's restaurant than the office. Cyril believed magic was 50 percent natural talent and 50 percent muscle memory, meaning that a childhood full of the iconic eatery's bread pudding would subconsciously influence her location. Romy wasn't sure if he was trying to make her feel better about her lack of skill or if his statement was truly grounded in science.

Viewing magic as a science might seem to be the opposite of all things supernatural, but as a scholar, Romy's mother had worked for years to prove her theory that all magical bloodlines shared the same cellular components. No preternatural researcher had found evidence to support her claim, but Romy hoped it was true. Perhaps one day, if all the races understood their similarities, their differences wouldn't create such division.

When Romy walked inside, she waved at her mother's secretary, Pearl. "Is Mom ready for me? I'm a little early."

"Let me check, hon. She was on a conference call a

few minutes ago." Pearl lifted the phone to her ear. "Dr. Delacroix, Romy's here. Yes, ma'am. I'll tell her."

Romy heard the door unlock. "Let me guess. She wants me to get her some water?"

"How did you know?" Pearl chuckled.

"Mom's a predictable woman." Romy thought about the truth of that statement as she stepped into the kitchen and removed two bottles of water from the refrigerator. Her mother was not only predictable but also dependable and trustworthy—all qualities Romy hoped she'd inherited. Cassia set the bar high as the high priestess, and though following in her mother's footsteps wasn't Romy's dream life, she was determined to make the best of it.

"Good morning, Andromeda." Cassia accepted the water from Romy's extended hand, then gestured for her to sit on the couch. "I'm glad you came."

"Yeah, me too. I guess you know I've got a ton of questions."

Cassia folded her hands properly. "I suspected, yes. I'll try to answer each one to the best of my ability."

"Great. First, though, thanks for inviting me last night, Mom. You didn't have to, but it means a lot to me that you did." She swallowed a gulp of water. "I'm not anywhere near ready to take my place on the council or become the high priestess, but I'm trying. I promise."

“It was time, dear. Your father and I hope the experience helped you gain an appreciation for our heritage and, perhaps, sparked an interest in its pursuit.”

After pulling her legs beneath her, she grabbed a throw pillow and set it in her lap. “Yeah, I could say that going to High Council has made me want to know more about the coven, about everything, honestly. I know I haven’t been as eager as you would have wanted...”

Cassia smirked. “No, you haven’t. You’re stubborn, and when you think something should be a certain way, there’s no changing your mind. It’s a good quality to have if channeled correctly. But we can work with it. You have all the qualities needed to succeed me.”

“You believe that?”

“I do.” She didn’t hesitate.

“Even though I haven’t reached candescence yet?” Romy was wary of the answer. Cassia was painfully blunt and always honest, even when the truth hurt.

“Andromeda, do you realize you’ve never asked me how old I was when I changed?”

“I just assumed...”

“Assumed that because I’m the high priestess, I automatically had full control of my powers from birth?” Cassia scoffed. “Not in the least.”

Romy raised an eyebrow. She’d always seen her mother as all-powerful, all the time. Could it be that she, too, took longer to come into her gifts? "How old were you, Mom?"

"Twenty. Almost twenty-one. You are only a couple of months older than I was. I'm hard on you, Andromeda. We both know it. But if I didn't know what awaited you on the other side of candescence, I wouldn't bother. You are my firstborn, so by birthright, the position of the high priestess is yours, but make no mistake, if I believed you were not meant to follow in my footsteps for one second, I would alter the line of succession. The coven has done it once before, and it can be done again."

"With you and Aunt Selene, right?" Romy's voice was small, hushed. Discussions surrounding Daphne's choice to pass over her eldest in favor of her younger daughter had been forbidden by Cassia when she took over the coven. If she heard anyone—friend or foe—slander her sister, she'd banish them with no questions asked.

Cassia reached across her desk for Romy's hand. "It's all right for us to talk about what happened, Andromeda. You need to know because our history affects you, but it's not as dramatic of a story as you probably think. Selene simply wasn't leadership material. Your grandmother made several attempts to prepare her, but for whatever reason, Selene didn't excel where I did. The decision was difficult but necessary."

"Mom, Thora's better than me already. You know this. Maybe I should bow out now."

Cassia shook her head. "Preposterous. You have my faith and my favor, Andromeda Delacroix. I believe in you."

"I don't know what to say." She really didn't. Cassia wasn't one to offer compliments, even when people deserved them. She believed one shouldn't be rewarded for doing their job, so her approval was hard-won. "Thank you, Mom. I won't disappoint you or the coven."

A hint of a smile crossed her lips. "Of that I have no doubt."

"But I will question things, though," Romy added. "I need to if I'm to understand."

"Of that I have no doubt, also. Speaking of, let's go over a few of your most pertinent questions from last night, shall we?"

Romy straightened. Maybe she could find out more about Silvan and Bastian. Inadvertently, of course. Cassia would blow a gasket if she knew her daughter found any preternatural besides a witch attractive. It was a dangerous concept, but Romy liked the idea of being risky. "About the Rincewinds... why are they so, *like*, explosive? None of them listen, and they antagonize the others on purpose. Why is that?"

"Wolf packs function better with two leaders: a

packmaster and his mate. Asa's mate, Ylfa, passed away a while ago, and he hasn't been the same. Aside from that, he's always been passionate." Deep in thought, Cassia tilted her head. "Everyone was surprised when Mother recommended him as packmaster, but he's proved calmer than most. I'm concerned about his heir, though."

"Who's supposed to be his heir? The one you spoke with? *Silvan*?" Even saying his name made Romy feel scandalous and seductive.

"Yes," Cassia said evenly. "Silvan."

"He seems pretty hotheaded." Romy felt a flush creep into her cheeks and prayed her mother wouldn't notice.

"He is, very much so. The accusation was a premature, rage-filled mistake, but unfortunately, I can't ignore it. If a vampire did not kill Claude Rincewind, the sentence will stand."

Romy winced. She didn't want to think about Silvan dying. "And if a vampire did kill Claude?"

"Then in years to come, you, my dear, will have a considerably unruly and defiant packmaster to manage."

Lost in a daydream about all the ways she'd like to manage Silvan, Romy didn't hear her mother's inquiry.

"Andromeda?" Cassia tapped the table with her nails.

"Ma'am?"

"You zoned out on me. What were you thinking about?"

"Oh, just how awesome it is to get to know all these preternaturals." She kicked herself for not being quick enough to come up with a better explanation, knowing her mother's response before it even came.

"Darling, being the high priestess is an extremely heavy burden. I don't want you to miscalculate the work it takes to govern our council. I've had to reschedule all my patients this morning to deal with this Claude Rincewind situation. Through the years, I've missed out on so much with you and your sister. Remaining fair and unbiased can't be underestimated, and that's not an easy task when you're an opinionated Delacroix."

"I know, Mom. I *am* taking this seriously." After a pause, she asked, "So what do you think? Do *you* believe a vampire murdered him?"

"To be honest, no. I wouldn't say that to anyone who wasn't in our family, but I visited *Le Ville Marchlande* myself earlier this morning and saw video footage of the new vampires inside the residence at the time of question. Apparently, they're staying with Monsieur Marchland."

Romy couldn't allow her thoughts to wander again—not to Bastian and definitely not back to Silvan. Her mother was right. This was important. "And what about the pack? Did you go see Claude's body?"

"I sent your aunt and several PC agents, and they'll report back to me this afternoon at PC Headquarters. If you're not busy, you're welcome to listen in."

She brightened, unsure if it was because she'd be learning more about Silvan and his pack or High Council business. "I would. Thank you. So I have a question about the Rincewinds, and you don't have to answer if you don't want to."

"I'll do my best, dear."

"Were you scared when Silvan made the murder accusation? I saw you look at Dad." Romy asked tentatively, unsure if Cassia would offer a rare moment of vulnerability or scold her for asking.

"I was. Mostly because, as I've mentioned, the peace is fragile. At first, it starts with accusations, then actual murders, then war. And that's something none of us want. Asa is... broken. Not everyone feels he's still fit to lead since Ylfa died. And Silvan... he's a loose cannon, but they're even more married to tradition than we are. No matter how united they may appear, there is definitely dissension within the pack."

"Lycans and vampires really seem to hate each other." Romy pushed her curiosity a little further.

"More than you or I know. The Rincewinds, specifically, have a deep-seated hatred for personal and heritable reasons too vast for us to discuss today. So what about vampires? You must have your questions about them?"

Romy glanced at the clock. Cassia probably had a ton of things she needed to do, and sociology class started in an hour. "I do. I'll be quick."

"I'm always willing to discuss these matters with you, Andromeda. Especially now."

Happy for the vote of confidence, Romy formulated her next question. "Why do I get the vibe that vampires don't have many friends in the preternatural world?"

A faraway look entered Cassia's eyes. Romy couldn't pinpoint her mother's emotions, but she almost seemed ashamed. "No. Not many friends at all. Vampires prefer isolation from their own kind and other races as well. When several of them meet up, a power struggle is inevitable. You've heard the saying too many cooks in the kitchen? Well, that's how it is when clans gather. Every vampire wants to be in charge because they all believe their ideas are best, so they choose to live separately. On rare occasions, a leader has emerged and united the clans, but trouble has always followed. And by trouble, I mean death and destruction. For everyone's safety, Alizon forbade all vampires from assembling in groups greater than twenty."

"So basically, if Bastian wants a family reunion, tough shit?"

Cassia cracked a smile. "Basically."

"That's unfair, Mom. I mean, the Rincewind Pack has a ton of members. And I'm assuming no other preternatural race has that restriction."

"No. They don't. And I agree with you, Andromeda. Though unjust, it's a vital part of the treaty designed to keep the peace. Vampires have been treated like villains because *they have been the villains.* For millennia, they've laid waste to entire civilizations—not for survival but for sport. As apex predators, they are at the top of the food chain, and the only reason the coven is sovereign today is because our ability to work as a collective unit exceeded theirs. If given the opportunity, they can and will dominate us."

"Is that why vampires can't talk to witches directly? That was so odd last night with the faerie and Bastian."

"Yes. It is strange but necessary. This stems from a vampire's innate ability to charm through the sound of their voice. They can do this to anyone, but especially a witch. Their biological inclination is to control us. We aren't certain why—it simply is—so as a stipulation of the treaty for the Hundred Years War, vampires have to use interpreters any time they address a witch to ensure they won't attempt it."

Romy scrunched her nose. That wasn't what she wanted to hear at all, though an unwelcome thought of Bastian ruling over her quickly followed. "So vampires want to *rule* over us?"

"I don't know if they want to rule over us as much as they want what we have. Our blood intoxicates them. It's a natural high."

She liked the expanded explanation even less. "What about Bastian? Did he use an interpreter this morning when you visited him?"

"He did. He always will. Though Bastian is different. I don't require him to use one when we speak alone, yet he always has."

"What did you say to him yesterday after the council dismissed?" Romy wasn't sure why she wanted to know more about Bastian Marchland if he wanted to get drunk off her blood, but her curiosity bordered on obsession.

"I told him I was sorry Silvan's allegation wasn't rooted in facts. Considering the extreme penalty, I never thought Silvan would outright blame a vampire, but he surprised me."

"And what did Bastian via fairie girl have to say?"

Cassia chuckled, an unlikely sound coming from someone so serious. "He was kind. He's *always* kind. He understood how it could seem as if a vampire had committed the crime and even encouraged me not to pass such a harsh sentence for the false allegation. He's not like other vampires I've encountered."

"Hmm..." Was Bastian's understanding attitude an attempt to enchant Cassia in some way? Now that

Romy knew the truth, she had to keep her guard up around Bastian Marchland. Sexy as hell or not.

As if her mother could read her skeptical mind, she added, "Bastian has been through a great deal in life. His tremendously *long* life. He was alive during the Hundred Years War and knew our grandmother, Alizon. But those are stories for another time."

"Thanks for this, Mom." Romy couldn't wait to learn more about both lycans and vampires. She was even a touch excited to learn more about her future as a high priestess.

"Always, darling." Cassia stood and walked her to the door. "Oh, and by the way, Mr. Teche will be relocating to New Orleans tomorrow. I believe he'll be staying in the Warehouse District. We'll have a family dinner at Brennan's."

Romy gaped at her. "Holy shit, don't you think you should have led with that?"

Cassia's mouth twisted into a frown. "Andromeda Delecroix, watch your language."

"Sorry, Mom." Romy scowled. "But really, Dane's coming *tomorrow*? Don't you think I should've been given more than twenty-four hours to prepare?"

"No, I don't," Cassia said matter-of-factly. "It isn't like you're getting married tomorrow or even this year. You'll have to meet him sometime. He is your Chosen."

Her Chosen?

Her Chosen?

No, not *her* Chosen. The Coven's Chosen. Romy had no choice in the matter whatsoever.

With a quiet and submissive nod, she blinked back tears. She wouldn't let her mother see her cry.

CHAPTER 5

as rough as they seem

The headquarters of the Preternatural Constabularies existed more as a museum than a place to conduct business. Located at the bottom of Lake Pontchartrain, the museum was constructed purely of magic and housed more preternatural artifacts than anywhere else. Since fraternization was illegal, last night's High Council meeting had been Romy's only exposure to the other races. Ironically, her favorite places had always been the exhibitions involving lycans and vampires. And Alizon's Dusk Gardens, which she planned to visit after the meeting.

Today, she went straight to the beginning of the lycan display and a mammoth white pelt with black guard hairs. Until now, she'd never noticed its name: *Jonas Ragbulf. Packmaster of the Ragbulf Pack. Ancestor of Ylfa Ragbulf Rincewind.* Silvan's mother. Romy admired the colors of the coat, and as usual, her mind wandered to her lycan—the thickness of his fur. How dark it would be against her skin. How she'd like to watch him shift from the beast into the man. Would he retain his savageness? The bloodlust, the untamed ferocity? Would he devour her body? Feast on her flesh?

"They're even more impressive up close and in person." Romy's Aunt Selene flanked her side. An almost mirror image of Cassia, the only marked physical variance was instead of the traditional cherry-red hue common to the Delacroixs, Selene's hair was so black it was nearly purple. As far as other differences, like personality and demeanor, the two sisters couldn't be more diverse. Romy's mother was assertive and poised, demanding respect with a quiet but effective confidence, while Selene preferred to blend into the background. It was easy to see why Daphne altered the line of succession.

"Are they?" All Romy could think of was Silvan up close and personal.

"Mm-hmm. They aren't as rough as they seem."

Romy hoped her lycan was as rough as he seemed. His calloused hands palming her ass. His teeth nipping at her neck. The thought of him holding her down with his hard cock pressed firmly against her pussy was enough to drive her mad. Yet again, she had a problem between her legs. "You do a lot of PC business with the Rincewinds, don't you?"

"When necessary, yes. Asa and I have a good professional relationship for the most part."

"Do you know his son? Silvan?" She tried to sound nonchalant, but she burned within. An ache only satisfied with a wolf. Maybe a vampire? A wolf and a vampire? Geez.

"Hmm. You mean the Neanderthal?" Selene grunted. "Asa has his hands full with that one."

"What do you mean?" Edging closer, Romy wanted to hear everything she could about Silvan—the good and bad.

After a gesture to resume walking, Selene pointed at a wolf directly across from Jonas Ragbulf—a long and thin brown male. "What do you know of wolf history? Probably not much since this is the extent of your childhood exposure."

"Right. I've always found it kinda dumb, actually. I mean, shouldn't we get to know the other preternaturals because there's safety within numbers."

Selene smiled properly. "There's safety within your coven, dear. Nowhere else. Though some believe otherwise."

"Yeah..." Perhaps she shouldn't have been so candid with Selene. The last thing she wanted was for any elders to question her ability to lead. Or did she? Romy was torn between her duty as high priestess-in-training and her desire to break free and run. Maybe even run with the wolves. "So you were saying about that wolf across from Jonas?"

"Einar Tyr. Leader of the Bloodmoons. Originally, they were the warrior wolves for the Ragbulf Pack, but Einar turned them into assassins. After murdering Jonas's entire family and most of the pack, they attempted to murder Jonas. It was the single most bloody conflict in recent lycan history."

Romy scrunched her nose. "What does that have to do with Silvan?"

Selene's heels clicked on the marble floor, and she crossed her arms. "Silvan reminds me of Einar. His impulsivity. His savagery. His blatant disregard for your mother and the High Council."

"How do you know?" she spat, a touch too defensively. Why did Romy care that her aunt compared Silvan to some ruthless wolf? Why did this lycan matter so much to her?

"Oh, just conversations in passing with Asa and the theatrics I've witnessed during past High Councils. But I digress... it's time for today's meeting." Selene looked down at her watch. "And I believe we are right on time."

When they reached the exit, Selene held open the door for Romy, and together they entered the boardroom. "After you, High Priestess..." she mused with a gleam in her eye.

"Umm... not yet. I'm nowhere near ready."

"That's what this time is for, Ro. To learn and experience. Maybe even to fail. I have faith in you, Romy. Just like I had faith in your mother."

Romy noticed a hint of sadness in Selene's last statement, and she wondered how her aunt must have felt, disappointing her family, her coven. She didn't seem too worse for the wear. Cassia had given Selene an exalted position within the High Council. She'd married, had Loren, and was Cassia's most trusted adviser. If Romy couldn't handle the pressures of being the next high priestess, at least she knew she'd always have a place at Thora's side.

"Ah, Andromeda... there you are." Cassia tapped the seat next to her.

"Found her perusing the lycan display." Selene tousled Romy's hair as she walked past.

Several other elders filtered in and joined them at the round table. Appropriately named the Dragon's Slab, the iridescent pearl table was composed entirely of a dragon's tooth, and Romy had always marveled at the different shades and shapes she'd found within. Dragons had gone extinct nearly three hundred years ago, and this relic was the only one of its kind.

With everyone seated, Cassia cleared her throat to

begin. "As this is an informal meeting, I'll skip the pageantry and give the floor to my sister."

"Thank you, High Priestess. I, along with Dr. Hiller"—she gestured to the man on her right—"conducted a thorough investigation of Claude Rincewind's body, and presently, we can't rule out a vampire. However, we found no other signs of vampires within the pack territory. We couldn't detect their scent, had no additional sightings, and obviously, there were no witnesses to the murder."

"And it was most assuredly a murder?" an older member asked.

"Unless Claude can rip out his own heart and drain his blood, then yes, a murder was committed." Dr. Hiller opened a folder and produced a handful of pictures for Cassia, who studied them briefly, then gave them to Romy.

She winced at the mutilated body of Silvan's uncle and wondered if Silvan had seen him, possibly even found him dead. Claude wasn't in his human form, but wolf. Matted gray fur and coagulated blood caked the sides of a cavernous hole where his heart should have been. His neck, obviously shaved for the necropsy, revealed the vampire's calling card of two perfect puncture wounds. His shriveled body was not from old age but because he'd been drained. Romy bowed her head and turned the pictures over before passing them along.

Seeing Claude somehow made Silvan even more real to her. Not in a physical way... though she was extremely aware of her feelings in that area, but in an emotional way. He was a wolf with a heart and blood, and a man who'd lost a beloved family member. She longed to comfort him.

"And what is the pack mentality, Selene?"

"They're all on edge, craving vengeance. Asa is doing what he can to pacify them, but the writing's on the wall... If Claude's killer isn't brought to justice, they'll go to war."

Cassia shook her head back and forth rapidly. "No. We'll find the killer. We cannot afford war. Monsignor Marchland is here with the two new vampires, and they're registering with the PC as we speak." She leaned over to her chief security officer. "Call the Fontenot Coven in Shreveport. They have a wizard who just retired from the FBI. See if he'll come down and help with the investigation."

"Right away, ma'am."

Romy heard bits and pieces of the remainder of the conversation, but her thoughts were single-minded. Bastian. Was. Here. And now, she had to find him. As soon as the meeting adjourned, she hugged her mother and aunt and sprinted to the registrar's office.

Through the glass windows, she spotted the same faerie who had helped Bastian at High Council, and on the young woman's right and left were two men. Pale skin. Distant expressions. Definitely vampires. But no Bastian. Instantly, her heart sank, but Romy couldn't understand why. One minute, she fantasized about Silvan's chiseled muscles and strong hands, and the next, she was lovesick over Bastian. Why couldn't she get excited about the man she was actually going to marry? She hadn't met Dane yet, but he was a dependable ticket to guaranteed sex.

Maybe that was the problem. No danger. No spontaneity. No passion. Romy Delacroix longed for that life... at least in her mind.

Romy searched for Bastian for half an hour, finally ending her quest at the gates of Alizon's Dusk Gardens. Magic channeled the moonlight, and the moonlight fueled the plant growth. Evening primroses, moonflowers, and chocolate daisies lined the paths, and farther out, row upon row of night-blooming jessamine, flowering tobacco, and the elusive Queen of the Night. She'd never explored the expansive grounds entirely but felt drawn to a certain area she'd never seen. Literally. Surrounding her now, the twilight shimmered, but there, only night. Romy always wondered what could grow in the blackness but could never think of an answer. Tonight, though, she heard a voice within her whisper *anything*. Anything can grow in the dark. Anything can find a way.

Gathering her resolve, she waded through the pond and into the unknown until the red water lilies faded to gray and black. Using her senses alone, she found the path next to the water. Romy looked up and then down to see purple sparkles around her. Stars? She wasn't sure. But she was certain she wasn't alone, and surprisingly, she wasn't afraid.

On impulse, she extended her hand into the murky darkness and felt a cool palm intertwine with hers. *Bastian.* She knew it was him like she knew her own name. Did vampires have a heartbeat because Romy could distinguish two hearts beating? Initially, their cadence was separate, level, and steady, but the longer Romy and Bastian remained physically connected, the more she could feel his core drumming in rhythm with her own.

If it was possible to see without eyes, Romy had all the vision in the world. She couldn't visualize Bastian before her. She could only feel him. But that was enough because they were one mind and one spirit at this moment, and through their connected palms, they'd fused as one body. It was the most intimate experience of Romy's life.

Then it was over.

And she was home, at Delacroix Manor, watching television with Thora. "Did... I... how did I... when did I come home?"

"Uh... like a few hours ago, dummy. You've been asleep for thirty minutes." Her sister didn't look in her direction.

"But... I... I was in the Dusk Gardens at PC Headquarters."

Irritated, Thora pressed pause on the remote and rolled her eyes. "Yeah... no shit, Sherlock. You and Mom went to look at the Queen of the Night without me. Jerks."

As Thora returned her focus to the program, Romy replayed the afternoon's events and couldn't determine any explanation except that she was losing her mind. How could she have been with her mother and then here, at home, if she was with Bastian?

She had to find out.

CHAPTER 6

lacy pink thong

Asa was a blind fool. Silvan felt like a traitor even thinking about his father in such terms, but if he saw how the man had changed, then what were others saying and thinking?

He hadn't always been that way. The Rincewind Pack had seen their best days under his smooth thumb of diplomacy, a rare skill among the mercurial pack and often underappreciated. Even Silvan sometimes thought Asa was soft. But a fool? Nah. Never.

Not until he'd put his diplomacy above his own people.

Silvan propped himself against a tree at the edge of the forest while the others talked shit about the Marchlands and Delacroixs. It was as much a precaution as a preference. Claude's death had changed something in him. He couldn't put his finger on it, but it meant something.

"We must allow the high priestess to conduct her investigation," Asa said in the same placating tone he used on babies. He gesticulated a hushing motion to calm the riled pack. "It is the way of the High Council, and one we must trust."

One of the older wolves stormed out of the gathered pack and toward the moss-covered log Asa held court from. "And why should we let that bitch Cassia decide *for* us how we handle an attack on *our* pack?"

My thoughts exactly, Silvan mused with an eye roll. He spat into the underbrush and closed his eyes, waiting for the farce of a funeral to end. Half the pack just wanted an excuse to draw vamp blood and didn't give a fuck about what had happened to Claude. The other half was nervous and scared. The accusation against the vamps had been an effective declaration of war, regardless of the truth.

"The council protects all of us. Wolves, witches, faeries, and yes, vamps," Asa said in a frustratingly reasonable tone. "But when they find out the truth, that the piece of shit bloodsuckers killed one of ours, they'll no longer have those protections."

"Open fucking season!" one of the young ones

called out and got everyone howling and beating their chests.

Piece of shit bloodsuckers. Well, it was an improvement from *let's play nice, shall we?* Wouldn't mean a damn thing if Asa couldn't grow a sack, though.

Silvan licked his lips and turned his head toward the night sky. The itch was almost insatiable, but shifting came at the end, where they would all come together for a hunt. More like a circle jerk of testosterone and useless bullshit.

He didn't used to feel so jaded about the pack, but he saw things differently as a man than he did as a boy.

"We should conduct an investigation of our own."

"Who says we can't sniff around in our own forests?"

"Who knows, might catch a fucking vamp where he doesn't belong."

On and on, they huffed and puffed, more useless banter, blah, blah, blah. Silvan slid his back along the rough bark to quell the itch to shift.

That's not the only fucking itch, though, is it?

Silvan had seen plenty of witches at High Council over the years, and they were all the same—high on their goddamn power, prim, proper, with shit that apparently smelled like fresh roses. But *this* one... Andromeda. Romy. It was almost like she didn't belong there at all. She was unsure of herself, and from the crude whispers passed along the pack later that night, he deduced she'd been slow to develop her magic. Romy Delacroix was a bit of a disappointment , and if Silvan could relate to anything, it was probably that.

Not that he would, or could, ever tell her that. But who had to know it was the wide-eyed little red-haired witch invading his thoughts when his hand stroked his cock?

He reached into his pocket and withdrew what he could only assume was a handkerchief. It was pink and... well, pink. He didn't give a fuck about that, but what he did care about was the utterly ripe and delectable scent left upon its silken threads by its former owner.

He wondered what Romy was doing at that moment.

Right on cue, his cock twitched.

After the hunt, he promised himself, but his enthusiasm for grieving in groups was considerably less than when he'd shown up that night. Soon, they'd stop beating their chests and fortifying their egos and shift as a single unit. They'd take down every poor creature who dared cross their ferocious path and feast until they passed out, delirious with bloodlust and waiting for oblivion.

"Fuck this," he hissed, slipping into the forest. He pressed the silk to his nose and inhaled deeply, memorizing the scent for his hunt.

No one called after him, but he waited until he was several yards away before shifting and bounding off.

It took longer than it should have to find her. He knew where the Delacroix mansion was, of course. Everyone did. It was vast, exceedingly decadent, and exactly the kind of digs he'd expect holier-than-thou witches to choose for themselves.

But Romy wasn't there.

His tracking was considerably stronger when in wolf form, but even in New Orleans, it wasn't safe for a wolf to run around on public streets. The last thing he needed was Animal Control on his ass. They already had a hard-on for the Rincewind Pack as it was. The pack was skilled at finding clothes on the fly, and Silvan had no trouble at all this time, leaping into a backyard where a line of clothes were drying. He slipped on a man's T-shirt and shorts that were not remotely his style. They were also tight as hell, but they'd be fine for the hour or so he needed until he was back in the woods.

But *fuck* could he smell her now that he was in her territory. It made his stupid little silk hanky feel like a drop of water to a man dying of thirst in the desert.

The scent ended on the sidewalk. She'd gotten into a car, most likely. *A fucking Town Car,* he thought with a smirk. Rich bitches were all the same.

Then why are you stalking this one?

Why indeed.

She could be anywhere at all, and by the time he figured it out, she'd likely be back home. He couldn't ask anyone he knew for help—even the thought of it made his skin crawl—but if she wasn't home...

The Delacroix undoubtedly had staff. Probably a whole damn stable of them.

The strength of her scent made his knees weak. He buried his face in his sleeve, then shook his arm away. He was better than this. A wolf without willpower wasn't even fit to run in a pack, let alone inherit one.

He glanced up at the looming mansion. Banana fronds swaying in the breeze pushed a lovely—relieving, really—wave of wisteria his way. It didn't erase the witch's scent but gave him a moment to think.

Silvan was no small man. There was no stealthing into any situation, regardless of what form he was in. But he *was* skilled in persuasion. And if he was caught by a member of the Delacroixs' endless staff, he could fast-talk his way out of it.

"Fuck it," he growled, creeping around the side of the house. It was the longest house he'd ever seen, and he wondered what the hell they needed all this space for. But the answer was they didn't. No one did.

There was movement beyond the long row of windows, but nothing to indicate he'd be walking into a circle jerk or a party. Things were even quieter around back, and as though fate's sense of humor was perfectly aligned to his, the back door was *open.*

A nearby delivery truck—*flowers* because they didn't fucking have enough of them on the damn plantation of a property?—revealed why. Even better. There'd be enough commotion he might not even need an excuse.

Silvan slipped inside and breathed deep. Her scent was goddamn everywhere. On everything. The force of it sent him careening into the screened porch, where he, quite embarrassingly, needed a moment to steel himself.

With *that* horrifying episode behind him, he entered a kitchen so small he knew there had to be another one somewhere else. Or two. Or three. Who knew with these rich bitch witches. A woman wearing a white uniform breezed past him without acknowledgment, and he took that as an encouragement to creep farther into the house.

Romy's scent heightened when he reached an elaborate stairwell that looked straight out of the movies. Silvan glanced around, ensured he was alone, and bounded up the stairs.

The hallway at the top was exactly what he'd imagined—a row of doors, enough for a small hotel, and walls lined with the most ridiculous portraits he'd ever seen. But he didn't care about them, or the doors, or any of it, because *holy shit* was her scent overpowering.

Get ahold of yourself.

Shaking it off, Silvan tried to restrain himself as he followed his instincts. As soon as he entered the bedroom, he was nearly knocked back. It wasn't just that her scent was every-fucking-where, either.

Who the *shit* liked this much turquoise?

He swept through her room, examining anything that might...

Might what?

Why was he even there?

Why wasn't he out hunting with the pack, bad mood and all?

Even as he thought these things, he rifled through her desk and dresser and opened her laptop. Password protected, of course. Next to it, though, was a diary, and he didn't think twice about opening it.

"Bah," he muttered when he realized it was an appointment diary. But just as he was closing it, he caught the date. Today. *Dinner with Dane. Brennan's. 7 PM. Just go ahead and kill me now.*

"Brennan's, eh? Fucking bluebloods." He slammed it shut, but his disgust had dulled. He knew where Brennan's was. Had eaten there a few times. They wouldn't let him in, dressed as he was, but...

Are you really going to pretend you're not gonna follow her?

A growl rippled from deep within, building until he had no choice but to release it into his arm.

He started to storm out but paused, thinking. Then he backtracked to her dresser.

And pulled out a lacy pink thong.

"Mine," he grunted and left.

CHAPTER 7

the burden of responsibility

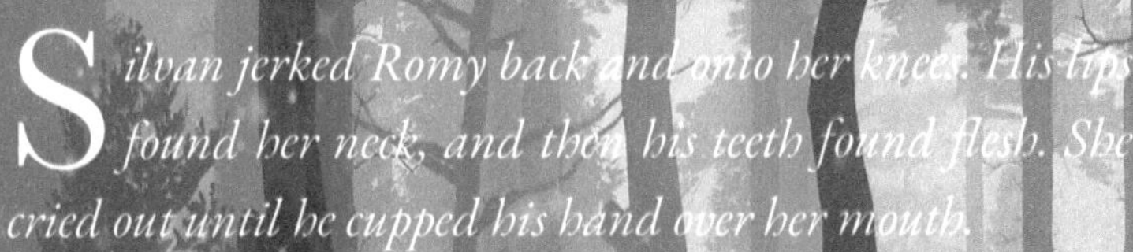

Silvan jerked Romy back and onto her knees. His lips found her neck, and then his teeth found flesh. She cried out until he cupped his hand over her mouth.

"Quiet," he demanded. "Not one single sound. Nod if you understand."

Romy obeyed but wondered what would happen if she didn't. Would he punish her? Would he force her to comply?

*His touch traveled from her neck and shoulders, arms, waist, then to her breasts, where he rolled a nipple exactly the way that drove her wild. "*This *is mine."*

Instinctively, Romy spread her legs as an invitation and reclined into Silvan's lap.

"And this *is mine," he growled. With expert precision,*

his fingers parted her, finding her desire. Using lingering, soft circles, he took her higher and higher and higher...

Ahead, a man waited in the shadows, yet Romy could hear his whispers as if he was as close as Silvan. Then she felt his palm press into hers.

Bastian.

"You *are mine, Andromeda Delacroix. You've always been mine. And I am yours."*

A burst of pain spread over Romy's shin, and she blinked rapidly, adjusting to the light and reality. Then she turned a deep shade of red. She wasn't with Silvan or Bastian. She was with Dane and both their families at dinner. At *Brennan's*, no less. Awesome.

"Andromeda Alesia Delacroix? What's going on?" her mother bellowed. "Can you hear me?"

Another sting to her shin. "Earth to Romy. Hey, weirdo, wake up!" Thora waved and stuck out her tongue.

"Oh shit, I'm sorry." Mortified, Romy covered her mouth. "I'm sorry for saying *shit*."

Cassia rolled her eyes and sighed in long-suffering exasperation. "I apologize for my daughter. I assure you she's not always so crass and aloof."

Dane's mother, Rosemary Teche, pursed her lips into an uncomfortable half smile and set her napkin down.

"Come on, Mom, you know I say *shit* all the time."

Dane patted his mother's back and winked at Romy. His father, Percy, attempted to conceal a chuckle but was unsuccessful.

Rosemary's eyes widened at her husband and son. "Dane, how rude! Both of you. Best foot forward, remember?"

"I think my *lost-in-a-daydream* granddaughter has blown that out of the water." Daphne laughed to ease the mood. "How about a realistic foot forward? We're all going to be family, right? Might as well let it all hang out."

After a few seconds of lighthearted conversation, the group relaxed and turned their attention to the jazz band strolling past them.

"Thank you," Romy mouthed to Dane, and he nodded in acceptance. Dane Teche. Her Chosen. He wasn't bad looking at all. In fact, he was handsome in a bookish sort of way. His exceptional intelligence had already been established. But neither of those things would make him a good husband or friend.

What instantly set Dane Teche apart was his willingness to make a fool of himself so Romy wouldn't be the only one embarrassed. And in Romy's eyes, that was worth more than all the good looks and brilliant minds in the world.

. . .

An hour later and finally rid of their families, Dane and Romy perused the Frenchman's Art Bazaar. She paused to look at an abstract painting filled with shades of blue. "I think the artist is trying to convey exasperation in this one."

"I see disappointment." Dane pointed at a ridge of darker tones. "The fade into black screams 'I'm pissed at the direction this is going.'"

"I can see that." Romy glanced at the table and snickered when she read the description. "We were both wrong. *Sapphire Bliss*."

"Ha... by a long shot, huh? We must be projecting our own feelings onto the painting, but I guess art's about interpretation, isn't it?" Dane nudged her shoulder.

"Totally."

They regarded the artwork again, then resumed their stroll. "So... disappointment. What are you disappointed about?"

"What are you exasperated about?" he countered.

"I asked you first." Romy appreciated their banter and, minus the awkwardness at dinner, had enjoyed getting to know Dane.

But enough to *marry* him?

Not that she had a choice in the matter.

Boldly, he took her hand and led her to a nearby

bench. "Are we gonna be honest with each other? Completely honest, I mean?"

"Brutally honest is always my preference. I don't want it any other way with us."

Nervous sweat trickled on his brow, and Romy could tell he'd been dreading this discussion. It wasn't at the top of her list either, honestly. "Being your Chosen is the ultimate honor. I don't want you to think I'm ungrateful."

Romy cocked her head. "I hear a big *but* coming on..."

"*But...*"

"There it is."

They laughed, and his tension faded. "But this isn't where I want to be. Going to law school, settling down here in New Orleans."

"Where do you want to be?"

After a deep inhale, Dane sighed. "New York. I've played the violin since I was a kid. 'Becoming well-rounded' is what my mom said, but I loved it and practiced every free moment I had. In college, I was first chair in the orchestra and played for the Baton Rouge Symphony. For shits and giggles, I applied to the Manhattan School of Music to see if I could make it... and got accepted. Didn't think I would."

"Wow."

"I'm sorr—"

"Don't be sorry, Dane." She cut in. "*Please* don't be sorry. I'm not into this arrangement either. This high priestess job isn't exactly something I'll excel at, so don't be sorry for not wanting a life forced on us both. *I'm* sorry for you and your dream. That really sucks. Is there any way you could still go?"

His head shook. "I turned them down at the beginning of the summer. It's too late."

"Damn," she said, looking down. "That's depressing."

"Yeah it is, but Romy, I'm going to honor my commitment. You need to hear that. I'm someone you can depend on. As a husband and a helpmate." His voice brimmed with sincerity and a conviction that compelled her to believe he meant every word.

For a moment, they sat quietly, the burden of responsibility to their family and the coven weighing on their shoulders. Would she and Dane ever embrace their calling, or were they doomed to resent it? Romy doubted divination would be part of her candescence gifts, but predicting the future was irrelevant. She'd make the best of this situation. Her attitude was the only thing she had complete control over.

"Wanna start with friendship?" She peered into his kind chocolate eyes. Behind them, she saw the same determined fire she felt within herself.

"Wanna start with a snow cone?" Dane countered as he pulled her up to stand next to him.

"Okay, now you're speaking my language." Romy clapped her hands together and fell in beside him.

After they joined the line, he removed his wallet. "What's your favorite flavor? I peg you as a Tiger's Blood kind of girl."

"Wedding cake, actually. No pun intended. Not yet, anyway." She gave his arm a playful punch. "What about you?"

"Almond Joy." Dane's hand went up for a high five. "Our marriage's foundation is our love of coordinating flavors. Hashtag winning at life."

Romy couldn't help but grin at his silliness. At least they had that in common.

While he went to the counter and placed their order, Romy wandered down a nearby alley to admire an indigo bougainvillea beginning its slow climb up a wrought-iron trellis. It was empty, a nice reprieve from an intense day.

Out of nowhere, a peculiar sensation started in her chest and spread throughout her body. She looked to her left and right, conducting a full-circle search. Only the oblivious patrons strolled by on the street she'd come from. But she could *feel* the undeniable force of someone's gaze. She knew she was being watched. She wasn't scared. Instead, she was even more turned on now than she was the night of the High Council.

Taking cover behind the trellis, Romy unbuttoned her shirt and undid the front clasp of her bra, exposing her breasts to the warm night air. Her hand slid into her shorts, and she braced against the iron, readying for her release. She didn't dare close her eyes. No. She wanted to see whose eyes were on her. Purple petals fell into her hair and onto her chest as her pace quickened. She imagined palming the ass of her unruly lycan, the salty taste of his arousal on her tongue. And between her legs? Bastian. Blood trailed a thin line down his chin from the bite mark on her inner thigh as her sex begged for more. She would let Bastian drink his fill of her blood, and Silvan... he could feast on her body. Romy bit her lip to muffle the sound of the orgasm.

Pleased, she slid her finger into her mouth and tasted herself, knowing someone remained fixated on her every move. She wanted them to see.

The only question in Romy's mind?

Was it a man?

Or beast?

Or both?

CHAPTER 8

summon the healers

Romy enjoyed her walk with Dane along Frenchmen, so much so she decided to invite him back to the Delacroix Manor. She was still riding the high of great conversation—not to mention her little interlude—and wasn't ready for it to end.

Dane had wandered down the alley with their snow cones, approaching with an odd look on his face. He'd reached into her hair to remove a bougainvillea petal, then turned his head to the side in curious inspection. Romy didn't know if he was pleased or puzzled, but the swell in his pants suggested he suspected… something. She'd half expected him to make a move—which she would have respectfully declined—but he hadn't said a word. A perfect gentleman.

Romy wondered if she'd ever feel the same passion for Dane as she inexplicably did for Silvan and Bastian. Even thinking about her strange attraction made her feel silly. She'd seen them once, yet both had assaulted her senses, dominating her thoughts, her body, and perhaps even her heart.

Now, *that* was silly. Love at first sight with not one but *two* forbidden men? Still, she couldn't deny the overwhelming compulsion to trace the sinewed muscles of Silvan's chest or spend the night in Bastian's bed.

Her sister's giggle reminded Romy to suppress yet another fantasy and return to the Monopoly game Thora had challenged them to. Her grandmother's description of her was on the mark. Since the night of the High Council, Romy had been perpetually *lost in a daydream*.

"That'll be six hundred bucks." Thora's chest puffed with pride as she squinted at the remainder of Dane's cashflow, a single one-hundred dollar bill. "And bankruptcy for you."

"You're cheating. Gotta be." With a playful flick of his wrist, Dane flung the paper money in her direction. He shook his head. "Witches."

"Nuh-uh. Scout's honor. Ask Romy. Daddy taught..." Thora paused to take a deep breath. "Daddy taught us to treat every property like it was as important as Boardwalk. By themselves, the streets are weak, but combined, they can win a game."

He frowned. "Good thing I like mops because you just wiped the floor with me."

"Wowww... that was..." Romy scrunched her nose at his dad joke.

"Terrible?" Dane finished.

"So... totally... terrible."

"My *punny-guy* charm's wearin' you down, baby."

With a hand cupped over her mouth, Thora leaned over to her sister and whispered loud enough for Dane to hear, "So will my nieces and nephews be more or less dorky than their dad?"

Before Romy could respond, Thora clutched her chest in panic. Her face was arrested in horror as she clawed at her throat, not breathing.

"Thora? Are you okay?" Romy watched the young girl's lips change from rosy pink to blue. Her chest heaved, but she couldn't speak. Something was terribly wrong. "Thora!"

The young girl bobbled back and forth. Had it not been for Dane's quick thinking, she would have face-planted onto the hardwood floor.

"I've got her. I've got her." He guided her to the couch.

"Thora?" Cassia called from upstairs. Unsurprisingly, she'd sensed her daughter's distress. "Romy, what's going on?"

"Mom! Dad! Come now!"

Less than five seconds later, her parents had joined them downstairs. Cyril was on the phone with the coven doctor while Cassia tended to Thora.

"She's burning up, Andromeda." Cassia pressed a palm to Thora's forehead. "Get me some cool towels."

"We don't know how it started," Cyril said into his phone. "They were playing a game... and what happened, Ro?"

Romy couldn't think. This had to be a bad dream. "She... she couldn't breathe. Grabbed her chest and almost passed out."

"Did you hear that, Dr. Bryant? Okay. Yeah. Come now." Cyril gestured to Dane. "Can you get your mom too?"

He nodded. "Done. She and Dad have just left the hotel. She'll be here in ten."

Dane's parents arrived only minutes before the coven doctor. Thora had worsened with each grueling second that passed. She'd vomited an orange substance with the consistency of bile, and her muscles had gone rigid. Worst of all, she'd lost consciousness, though Romy thought that might be a small mercy for poor Thora, who had never looked more scared.

Upon realizing the seriousness of the situation, Dr. Bryant called the entire medical team.

Romy fought tears as she stroked Thora's hair. "I'm so sorry, Thor. I love you. It's going to be okay. They'll figure it out and fix this."

"They need to perform some tests, Andromeda," Cassia said, sharp enough to snap Romy's attention her way. Medical personnel filtered around them in a flurry of crisp linens and leather bags. "Let's allow them to do their jobs in peace."

"I'm not leaving her, Mom," she countered with the same brusque tone. "*Somebody* needs to be with her." The implication that Cassia wanted to leave was unwarranted, but Romy wouldn't apologize. At least not until Thora was safe.

Cassia started to reply but paused when Dane's hand settled on Romy's shoulder.

"My mom will come and get us if anything changes. I promise you," Dane said gently. "Mom's got her."

"But what if... she..." The statement caught in her throat. A world without her sister wasn't a world at all.

"She won't, Romy. She's not," he reassured with such fervor that Romy almost believed him. A nurse carefully reached between Thora's head and Romy's arm to place a sensor for the EKG machine. Romy *was* in the way, and as long as Dane's mom would come get them, she'd relent and wait outside.

Reluctantly, she took Dane's outstretched hand and followed him into the next room.

Thirty minutes later, Dr. Bryant met with the Delacroixs to give the prognosis. Rosemary stood at his side.

"Some of the lab work came back. Her white count and sed rate are dangerously high. The fact that she's a preternatural is the only thing saving her right now." He waited for the family to process the information. "If she were mortal, we'd be in an entirely different situation, and I'll be honest, that's both fortunate and unfortunate."

"How so?" Cyril asked. He sounded there but also not.

"Our systems are enhanced because of the magic in our blood, and this buys us a small amount of time... yet..." Clearly, Dr. Bryant didn't want to continue.

"Go on," Cassia pressed.

"*Yet...* I have never seen a case like this. Not once." He turned to Rosemary. "Neither has Dr. Teche. No exaggeration is involved when we say neither of us has ever dealt with anything like this. Thora's metabolic composition is altered. She is completely changing. The process is slow, but it's almost as if she's turning into another species."

Cassia's eyes widened, but she didn't speak.

"How is this possible? Has she ingested something? Or is this specific within Thora herself? Candescence wouldn't trigger this, would it?" Cyril paced the room as if movement alone would generate a solution. Then he answered his own question. "No... I'm grasping at straws here."

"Anything is possible, Cyril, but it's unlikely. There's no way to know whether the increased power would help or hurt. We'd need time to study it... but you don't have time."

"What's the recommendation?" Cassia asked, her voice mechanical, robotic.

"I'm sorry to say this, but call the healers."

The reality of those words hit Romy with a force that pushed her into the back wall, and she couldn't remain quiet any longer. "Call the healers? Call the motherfucking *healers*? You just got here, and you automatically know Thora's a lost cause within an hour? How about getting a second opinion? Healers are for old witches, for the terminally ill."

No one spoke. No one wanted to say it. But Romy would—for Thora. She would do anything for Thora. "She's not a lost cause. She's worth more than five minutes of trying."

Cyril reached for Romy's arm, but she batted him

away. “Sweetheart, you know our laws. We have to release her to The One and The Only.”

“Fuck our goddamn laws, Dad.” Her stare centered on her mother. “And fuck our stupid coven for believing in a deity that thinks it’s okay to just let somebody go without trying. Thora is twelve and healthy.”

“You know it’s more complicated than that, Andromeda.”

Cassia seemed to rise with each word, but Romy knew it was an illusion used to intimidate. The high priestess would never back down, but neither would she. “Call your fucking healers. Let them lay hands on her, but I swear to you if something happens to Thora, it’s on *you*, Mom.”

Cassia’s face bloomed with red. “Don’t threaten me, Andromeda.”

She took a step even with Cassia. “Take it however you want. I don’t give a fuck. But I will burn hell to the ground if my sister dies.”

“You can’t even light a candle. How do you expect to do anything more?” Cassia hissed. Regret washed over her face, but the damage had been done.

At least she knew what her mother really thought of her.

“Andromeda... forgive me. I’m sorry. I had no right.”

Romy’s hand went up, creating a barrier between herself and Cassia. “No,” she whispered. “Stop.”

After pushing past the medical personnel, she knelt beside Thora, still unresponsive, and kissed the top of her head. "I promise we'll figure this out, sis. *I'll* figure this out. I love you."

Then she ran.

UNSURE OF WHERE TO GO OR WHAT TO DO, Romy turned left off Coliseum and drove toward the river. At the first stop sign, she pounded her steering wheel and screamed. How could her parents just give up? How could they turn their backs on their own child? Romy knew they loved her and Thora. Their devotion had been consistent and steadfast throughout her entire life, and perhaps that was what disturbed her most. Their neutrality violated every single thing she believed about Cassia and Cyril Delacroix.

The coven's laissez-faire philosophy stemmed from their belief that whatever transpired—good or bad—was the will of The One and The Only. While she'd seen it in action with the elderly and heard of instances when they'd allow a younger, chronically ill member to pass, she never dreamed her parents would permit the practice with their own daughter.

Fuck. That.

And fuck them for allowing it.

Her phone lit up with several texts, most from

Cassia, apologizing. Two from Loren, the first inquiring about why the healers were called for Thora and the other saying she'd heard the news. Another from her grandmother, who sent an excerpt from one of their ancient, sacred texts: *should any of you find yourselves or those you love on the brink of death, summon the healers within the covens and believe in the will of The One and The Only.*

Bullshit. Bullshit. Bullshit.

Furious, Romy almost tossed her phone on the floorboard but decided to open a message from Dane.

Dane: where'd you go? Just tell me, Romy, cuz I'm looking until I find you.

Romy really didn't want company, but she didn't want to be alone either. She checked the clock. 9:15 p.m.

Romy: meet me at The Fly.

TEN MINUTES LATER, ROMY LOOKED UP FROM the river's edge to see Dane. He set a book at her feet.

"*Divina Maledictio.*" She drew the last word out in slow syllables. "What am I looking at?"

"It means The Divine Curse. Dr. Clive Rice, one of my mom's mentors, wrote this. From what I understand, Dr. Rice collaborated with several other preternaturals to compile a comprehensive list of spells ranging from menial hexes to destroying entire cities.

He... um... disappeared... because he disagreed with the High Council's rules about interaction between the races. And for obvious reasons, this book is banned."

"I'm guessing my dear grandmother had a hand in that." The words left a bitter taste in her mouth. Romy knew the High Council had its flaws, but she'd never seen evidence of the coven's totalitarianism before that evening.

She shouldn't be surprised. Her world mandated conformity.

Dane kept his focus on the ripples of the water.

"You don't have to confirm it. I know she did. That's probably why she never supported my mom conducting excessive preternatural research. Sometimes I get the feeling that our coven doesn't care for anybody other than those like us. And if that's the case, then we have no business presiding over any council." She ran her fingers over the worn leather volume and brought it to her nose. "Old books. I love them."

"Me too." Dane leaned down and inhaled.

"I know your mom took a big risk, so please tell her that regardless of what happens, I appreciate it. The secret stays with me."

"Thanks for that reassurance." He flipped over to a dog-eared page. "This is where she suggested we start. Fenrir's Rose. Supposedly, it's lethal for most witches to consume in its natural state, but an altered form can be used to heal. With this, we'd have a fifty-fifty shot of healing Thora. If she ingested it, she could die. But she could live too."

The odds were shit, but it beat sitting around and waiting for the worst to happen. "Where do we find it?"

"From what Mom said, the plant is usually found near the Lycan Woods. She didn't know why, but it seems to favor growing near the wolves." Dane frowned. "Doesn't seem like the best idea, but it's all we have. I'll go with you if you want."

Romy's breath hitched in her throat. The Lycan Woods. Wolves. *Silvan*. "I can be ready in the morning."

WHEN DANE HAD FOLLOWED HER HOME AFTER their meeting at The Fly, Romy didn't go inside Delacroix Manor. Instead, she waited until his headlights disappeared, then returned to her car.

Against her better judgment, Romy slipped inside Alizon's Dusk Gardens at PC Headquarters.

Now, she waited in the darkness. For what, she couldn't say. She still didn't have answers about what happened the last time she was in the gardens, and in light of Thora's situation, she'd pushed it to the back of her mind. Yet she longed to be here with him. He was here. He'd been at The Fly. If Romy thought about it hard enough, she could recall *feeling* him throughout most of her life.

Did that make him a stalker?

Did that put her in danger?

No. Never.

This man, this *being*, had known Romy for eternity, and she'd known him. He was as familiar as her reflection in the mirror and exactly the solace she yearned for.

She knew there would be no words. Only feelings. She knew she wouldn't see him. Darkness was the only witness to their union. As soon as Romy waded through the pond and into the black, she felt his hand intertwine with hers.

Bastian.

Bastian.

His name was a balm spreading over her fears and insecurities. He sensed what had happened with Thora and was burdened—mostly because of Romy's own pain, but there was something else. Something more. A brother. Bastian had a brother who died in the most tragic of circumstances. Romy was unsure how, but the grief was palpable. It wasn't the same as what Romy faced because Thora was still alive, but Bastian understood the depth of love she had for her sister and the fear of losing her.

Instinctively, Romy laid her head on his shoulder and closed her eyes. She didn't care that she'd be at home when she opened them again. She didn't care if this was vampire mind control or if their interaction was forbidden. None of that mattered. The only thing of any consequence was their two palms pressed together in perfect union.

Bastian's grip tightened, and Romy relaxed, finally at peace.

CHAPTER 9

oops, i've accidentally mated with a witch?

Silvan had barely entered his father's house when Asa came barreling down the narrow hall of his shotgun cottage like a man with a vengeance.

The problem was that Asa wasn't quite vengeful enough these days.

"There you fucking are," his father growled. His flannel shirt practically bursted at his biceps, which rippled like violent waves under the thin fabric.

"Been hitting the weights, Dad?"

"I'm in no mood for your usual bullshit, Sil. In case you hadn't noticed, we have a murderer on the loose in our woods."

Silvan cackled in disbelief. "In case *I* hadn't noticed? You're the one on your knees for some fucking witches while they conduct their little 'investigation,' or whatever the fuck they're doing while we all sit and wait for them to feed us the truth."

"You're walking a fine line you don't want to cross," Asa said when they reached the kitchen. He pointed at the small round table by the window. Moonlight spilled over the center, illuminating the flaws in the old wood. "Sit."

"I'll stand," Silvan replied, crossing his arms defiantly. He almost hoped his father *would* punish him. At least it would dull the grief.

And your arousal over that pretty little redheaded witch.

Asa's brows fused. The thick vein in his neck was especially popping at that moment. "I wasn't asking."

Silvan wasn't sure why he pulled the chair out and dropped into it. He was in the mood for blood. For sex. Both, ideally. At the same time...

A fight would suffice, and his father seemed ready for one.

Until he bent in obedience to his alpha, Silvan hadn't realized he wasn't.

"Right. So why didn't you shift with the pack at Claude's funeral?"

Silvan shrugged. "Didn't feel like it."

"Didn't feel like it?" Asa parroted, sounding like a spoiled tween girl. "Do you want to guess how often I don't 'feel like' doing something?"

"Not really, Dad, but you'll tell me anyway." Silvan stopped his eyes from rolling before he really sent Asa into a fury.

Asa slammed back in his chair with a confounded glare. "You're going to be the *alpha,* Silvan. Your smart mouth won't win any battles, but it will sure as shit start them."

"When I'm alpha, there won't *be* a council. Rincewind Pack will be done kowtowing to those hoity-toity bitches."

"You think that," Asa said, "like we all did. Every last alpha has big ideas about emancipation and going solo. But when you run with my paws, you'll understand war isn't so appetizing when you have the fate of the entire pack resting on your shoulders."

Silvan never wanted to be alpha for the precise reason his father was now proselytizing. He could lead. No problem. But politics? Nope. No, thank you. Smiling and playing nice-nice with Cassia Delacroix? Double nope.

Romy will be the high priestess when you're alpha.

Even worse, because then he'd never get her out of his head. Never get the sweet smell of her nectar out of his nostrils. The little whimper she made as she tried desperately to mask the moment she made herself come.

In public, no less.

Perhaps someone should send Mr. and Mrs.

Delacroix an anonymous letter about what their daughter had been up to.

"Did you hear a goddamn word I said, Sil?"

"I'm tired. Sorry." Silvan dragged both hands down his face. "Long night."

"Don't tell me about long nights when you were off on your own while the rest of the pack grieved together," Asa groused, but his salty mood had thinned. He rapped his knuckles against the table's edge. "I asked if any of those girls you've been bedding night after night have unearthed any sense of which one is your mate."

"My mate?" Silvan scowled. "I'm in no hurry for that."

"You're older than I was when I mated to Ylfa." Asa sniffed as though he could smell her. "The truth is, when I found out it was her, I almost ran away. Couldn't stand your mother, not back then. But the mate bond is strong. It's the most powerful form of magic running through Rincewood blood. You'll know when the time comes. There won't be any question about it."

Silvan knew all that but was happy not to have felt the "twitch," as some of the wolves called it. None of the women he'd bedded were mate material, which was the whole fucking point. He didn't *want* to get close to the suitable ones because God forbid...

A devastating thought jumped into his mind. "Have

there been pack members who felt the twitch with other preternaturals?"

"You mean, not wolves?"

Silvan nodded. A novel feeling crept across his chest, tightening.

"Well," Asa said with an upturn of his nose, "*that* is precisely why we don't interact with other races. Because yes, it does happen. It has happened. And it can never, ever happen again."

"Why?"

Asa blinked hard. "Why?"

"Yeah, why?" Silvan tried to sound casual, but an acrid taste crept across his gumline. "Does one of them spontaneously combust or something?"

"You're trying to divert me and doing a piss-poor job. You need a mate, Sil, and if the twitch doesn't happen soon... well, it may not happen at all. For some, it never does. Which means I'll be choosing your mate."

Unless I've accidentally mated with a witch? Oops? "Right." Silvan tried to swallow but couldn't get *her* out of his head. He'd never, ever looked twice at a witch before. Certainly never stalked one, went to her home, and...

To be fair, he'd waited to drop a load in her stolen panties until he got home. He wasn't a *complete* savage.

Asa's eyes drifted to the shelf under the windowsill. He shook his head with a sigh. Silvan saw what had snared him—a picture of Ylfa when she was Silvan's age. "I've been unbalanced for a long time, Son. Something snapped inside me when your mother was killed, and I've suffered for it. The pack has suffered for it. I could choose another mate, but what would be the point? You're the future of Rincewind, Silvan. Not me."

"You should, you know? Find another mate. It's what Mom would have wanted," Silvan said. He couldn't look away from his mother's portrait, either. She'd been such a beautiful woman, her lycan form sleek and dangerous. Silvan resembled her more than his roughneck father, and he often wished it weren't so. Every time he looked in a mirror, he saw her, and his head filled with stars of rage. A fucking vamp had killed her, just like a fucking vamp had killed Claude. And the pack hadn't done anything about it either.

"It's too late for me, Sil," Asa replied, his voice much quieter than before. The way he said it left a sour feeling in Silvan's belly as if they discussed two different things. "But your season is just beginning."

Silvan's sudden rage had no place in his father's somber reflection. He willed himself to calm. "When does the council convene next?"

"When Cassia Delacroix deigns to summon us," Asa quipped. Then he murmured, "Fucking bitch."

For a moment, Silvan saw the old Asa Rincewind, the fiercest wolf in the pack.

But then it was gone.

"That's all," he said with a dismissive hand wave. "You can go back to doing whatever the fuck it is you're doing. But you have until the end of the year to mate, or I pick one for you."

CHAPTER 10

what's a hot little witch doing in my woods?

Silvan had only agreed to take a patrol shift in the forest to appease his father and get the man thinking about something *other* than a mate for his son.

It wasn't that he didn't know the day would eventually come, but he'd hoped to delay it as long as possible.

Few things interested him less than sleeping with the same woman for the rest of his days. And besides, men remained virile well into their sixties and seventies. Why should he settle down now when he still had decades of fun ahead?

Silvan stopped at a stream to drink. Water *always* tasted better in his wolf form. Drinking was primal and innate like sex.

Great, now I'm thinking about the damn witch again.

He finished and bounded off. Deeper into the forest he went. The others would stay near the lake because Asa said Claude's body had been displayed for others to find and not hidden in the shadows. Fair enough, but Silvan didn't believe for a second Claude was killed where they found him. Wolves were always in that part of the woods, which weren't exactly prime hunting grounds for sick and twisted vamps.

His muscles screamed in excitement as he pushed his pace. Drool dripped from his mouth and sprayed the gloaming. He ignored the ache and used it as fuel, moving faster and harder than he had in months. Years. Soon, his paws barely hammered the ground at all, and he was flying, soaring over cypress knees, logs and bushes and rabbits.

You don't have to be that man.

Claude's wisdom. Claude's words. Claude's fucking *voice,* coming together to form a memory still too painful to fully dredge.

You are the man you were born to be, Sil. Others may be waiting for you to come into yourself, but that's their loss. You've already arrived precisely as you are. Our blood doesn't make mistakes.

Was that why he'd been killed? Because the vamps sensed he was different from the other wolves? Would those same differences make Silvan a target?

Well, I'm waiting for you fuckers, and oh, how I wish you would fucking try.

Silvan pushed on, but the heart had been sucked from his run. His legs slowed, his breathing metered. He eyed a large stump peeking from the forest floor and determined it was a good place to rest, but before he could make the climb, his ears perked.

Nothing.

No, he'd definitely heard it.

He waited, and then it happened again. Cracking of branches. Crunching of leaves. Quickly, in his head, he measured the distance of the stride, the width of the step, and the force of impact, and determined it had to be humanoid. But on the smaller side, so a child or a young woman.

The only explanation for a child to be this deep in the woods was if it was lost.

A young woman, though...

Silvan stilled. Breath held, he waited for the person to come closer. Even without actively inhaling, he knew the scent anywhere.

Her.

Before he convinced himself he was acting irrationally, he bounded out and landed in a squared stance. Romy's eyes flew wide, and her mouth formed for a scream, but he shook his wolf head, which was enough to give her the pause he needed.

Silvan's flesh ripped as he shifted back into his human form. He drank in her little scandalized expression and determined he'd be the cause of it again one day, with his head between her legs. When he showed her what a *real* orgasm felt like.

Romy's mouth grew wider and wider with each breaking bone and snapping tendon. She covered it when he was done and standing completely nude in front of her.

Her eyes traveled downward to the cock he did nothing to hide. He noted how long her appraisal lasted. Every millisecond was like a ring tightening around the base, increasing the swelling until he was ready to burst.

Grinning, Silvan crossed his arms. "What's a hot little witch doing in *my* woods?"

"I... I didn't... mean..." Romy's head passed back and forth in tiny, erratic shakes. "Can you put something on?"

He shrugged. "If you want to follow me back to the lake where I left my clothing."

"Where the other wolves are?"

"That's right."

"I don't think that's a good idea," she muttered, more to herself it seemed. She pursed her mouth and released a short breath. Her gaze fluttered to his cock, but she shook her head and tore herself away. "I think I'm a little lost."

Silvan took a deep sniff and picked up a scent that nearly sent him into a rage. It was that other witch, the boy who had been buying snow cones while she finger-fucked herself in an alley nearby. He didn't know much, but the Delacroixs were clearly engaged in their own witchy matchmaking. "Where's your boyfriend?"

"I don't have a boyfriend," she said quickly enough to send his brows up.

"No? Who was the man in the Quarter with you?"

"Oh, him... he's my..." She swallowed. "Friend. Maybe more if our mothers have their way."

Her chosen mate then, as he suspected. "And he just left you here, all by yourself, to toil alone in the deep woods?" Silvan, still grinning, angled sideways and leaned in. "Where *any* of us could be waiting? Hunting?"

Romy's neck danced with her escalating pulse. Her veins looked beautiful, ripe with delicious blood. Silvan understood a vamp's foul urge for the first time. "What are you hunting?"

"Killers." His nose twitched. "Are you a killer, Andromeda Delacroix?"

Romy pulled her long red hair away from her face and lifted her chin. "I'm sorry about your great-uncle, but that had nothing to do with me."

"So you know who I am?" The thought delighted him.

"Sil... Silvan Rincewind. Asa's son. Right?"

Silvan smirked. He ran his gaze over her soft, pale skin, perfect little jawline, and lean, milky neck. "How many other names did you remember from your first High Council, Andromeda?"

"Romy," she stammered. "You can call me Romy."

"Are we on such intimate terms already?" Silvan flicked his tongue along his lips—first the bottom, then the top. Her cheeks flushed a deep red, so he did it again. Another hard sniff and he detected exactly the scent he'd been after.

But there was another scent. One that killed his sex drive in an instant.

Grief.

"Why are you here, Romy?"

Her face crumpled in sorrow, and she quickly turned away, wiping her eyes out of his sight. "If my mother knew I was even talking to you..."

"I won't tell her," Silvan said. "You don't have to tell her."

"I shouldn't even *be* here. This was a mistake, a terrible idea. We've been searching for *hours*, and still, nothing—"

"Searching for what?" Silvan asked, drawing nearer. Close enough he could lick her tears away.

"It's my little sister," Romy answered finally. She kept her face adamantly turned away, but the effort hid nothing. He saw all her truths in her profile: fear, love, grief, hopelessness.

He couldn't explain the sudden urge to swipe all her troubles off the map.

"Your little sister..." Silvan urged. His heart beat faster, in time with hers.

"She could die if we can't find Fenrir's Rose," Romy blurted as though spilling a terrible secret.

Silvan cocked his head back. "Fenrir's Rose. There's none left in the forest and hasn't been for years. Who told you it was here?"

"Doesn't matter," she muttered. "It's *not* here. This is a waste of time. I should be holding Thora's hand, not running around looking for a silly flower. This is so dumb."

"Marécage Island. It grows there." Silvan grimaced at his sudden bout of foolishness. If he thought Asa was mad at him before, well, telling a witch where they'd moved the invaluable plant was probably enough to get him excommunicated for a few months.

Romy looked up at him with a hopeful blink. "Where's that?"

Tell her it's unreachable. Tell her you were wrong. Tell her anything but the truth. "I could take you."

"You could?" She watched him closely. Her pouty mouth opened and closed. "And why would you do that?"

Yeah, fuckhead, why? "You said she'll die without it?"

Romy bit her lip and nodded.

"What's wrong with her?"

"We don't know. Maybe a curse? Maybe an illness? She's..." She turned around, searching. "Ah, God, where is Dane?"

"Ditch the nerd," Silvan said. His hand snaked out and wrapped around her forearm. She looked down at it with a little gasp. "And I'll help you."

"Then tell me why." She yanked her arm away with a defiant look that made him so hard he winced. "Wolves hate witches. How do I know you won't lead me into a trap and kill me?"

"You don't," Silvan said, laughing in spite of the somber pall. "But your sister is just a kid, yeah? Kids are innocent."

Romy aimed a soft chuckle at the ground. "And us? What are we?"

"Old enough to bear the burdens," Silvan answered. They both went quiet. "We can't do it now. Poindexter back there will be looking for you. Wouldn't want him bringing a fucking search party and starting a war."

"I'm scared one is coming anyway..." Romy sighed and looked behind her again. "My mother would kill me if she knew I was talking to you. To *any* other preternatural."

"Do you always do everything your mother tells you?"

"Well, I try," she said with an offended scowl.

"I've heard plenty of stories about Cassia Delacroix in her prime. She wasn't always so fucking proper."

"What? What does that mean?"

"Nothing." Silvan braced a hand on a nearby tree. "Need to decide now before your boyfriend comes back. If he sees me, I'm done."

Romy nibbled her lip and tapped one of her sneakers on the leaves. "When, then?"

Silvan killed his forming grin. It wasn't appropriate in the midst of talk about a dying child, but neither was his raging hard-on—which was much more stubborn. "You remember how you got here?"

She nodded.

"You could get here again by yourself? Don't need a babysitter?"

"Of course I don't need a fucking babysitter!" Her eyes flared in indignant anger.

"Yo," Silvan snapped, patting the air. "Keep your damn voice down, princess. Unless you wanna wake the *really* scary wolves."

"Whatever," she muttered. Her eyes swept his engorged cock again, lingering. He had half a mind to grip it and offer it up to her as dessert. She seemed to almost tear herself away to look up. "I can find my way back on my own. I don't need help. Just tell me when."

"A quarter after two," he said, locked in a battle with himself he'd lost before he even started. "Come alone, or don't come at all."

"How do we get to this island?"

"You'll see." Silvan sniffed hard. "Your boyfriend is about a hundred yards east of us. Follow this tree line, the ruts in the old path, and you'll find him in a few minutes. When you see him, you say—"

"Nothing," Romy said, shoulders back. "I say I got lost and found my way back, and that's all."

"That's all."

"You really won't tell me why you're helping me?"

Silvan grinned. "Only if you tell me why you thought about me as you touched yourself in that alley."

Romy stepped back as shock settled into her delicate features. "I don't know what... you're talking about."

"I can smell it on you now, too." He closed his eyes and inhaled. "If you leave now, you'll have plenty of time to scratch that itch, princess. Get it out of your system. Just don't go overboard and fall asleep. My offer to help is a one-time deal."

"You're disgusting."

"I can be whatever you want," Silvan said. He grew serious. "Go. I'll see you in a few hours. *Alone.*"

"You promise you'll be here? That you won't hurt me?"

"I make no promises," Silvan answered. He raked his tongue along his teeth. "But it seems like I'm all you've got. So come. Or don't."

"Two," she said, backing away. Her eyes remained locked to his. "Alone."

Silvan nodded, holding her gaze until she finally turned and disappeared into the forest.

When she was gone, his hand moved to his cock, drawn by feral instinct. He stroked the massive length, the unruly thickness that sent a blinding wave of pleasure to his head with every full pass. His knees turned to jelly, his palm slapping the tree.

Silvan came so hard his eyes swum with stars. He bowed, his thighs flexing, his cock spurting so much cum he could have drowned the little witch in his spend.

It was that thought that had him coming a second time.

And then a third.

What the fuck are you doing?

Claude. His father. Himself. The voice was the same this time.

What the fuck *are you doing?*

"We'll see," he grumbled and then shifted back into his wolf form, feeling ravenous and utterly alive for once.

CHAPTER 11

a favor

Romy had lied to Silvan. Not because she wanted to but because it was the proper thing to do. Years of being the perfect young woman—virginal and respectful—had triggered her to tell him he was disgusting. And she didn't think anything about Silvan Rincewind was disgusting.

He was bold. Lewd. Pretentious. *Cocky. So fucking cocky*, with his magnificent cock as the operative part of that word, and she couldn't resist the urge to stay and watch him. As expected, his hand had gone straight to his groin, and he'd stroked himself to an even longer and harder length. Romy's finger had moved inside her pussy in tandem with his strokes, and when he came three motherfucking times, she came too. He'd drown her with that cum, but what a way to go.

Nothing could have prepared her for the shock of meeting him in the woods. It was always a possibility—the Lycan Woods were his home—but he caught her off guard. Perhaps even more astounding was him engaging her, first as a wolf and then as a man. The wolf was impressive, and the shift was fucking amazing, but the man? The man was incredible. No matter how she'd tried to avert her eyes from the rock-hard member standing at full attention, she couldn't. That cock was a fucking magnet, and the only thing she could think about was the exquisite pain she'd feel as he pushed the head inside her pussy.

He'd sensed her arousal. More, he'd seen her in the alley. Romy had known it was him. She'd known Bastian was there too, and confirmation that Silvan saw her with her hand between her legs was the ultimate aphrodisiac.

"Sorry we couldn't find it today, Romy." Dane's fingers lingered on the middle of her back as they walked inside the Delacroix Manor. "We can go again tomorrow if you want. Maybe to a different part of the woods?"

"Sure..." Romy agreed, though she hoped to find Fenrir's Rose with Silvan in the early morning. He'd never told her exactly how he knew where the plant was or how they would get to whatever island he mentioned. And she didn't care. As long as it led to Thora's healing. "Thanks. I really appreciate you."

Dane's face brightened. "Anytime."

"Oh, Andromeda, there you are. I've been texting you." Cassia leaned over the banister from upstairs. Likely, she'd come from Thora's room. "Called you too."

When Romy pulled her phone from her pocket and saw her mom's missed call and unanswered texts, she immediately regretted getting sidetracked with Silvan. Thora was fighting for her life, and Romy just *had* to see the big lycan jack off. "Is Thora—"

"The same." Cassia interrupted. "I needed to speak with you about a favor."

Dane backtracked to the door. "That's my cue to make like a banana and split. I'll check you—"

"Stay, Dane." She cut in again. "This pertains to you as well."

They exchanged puzzled glances and sat on the couch as Cassia came downstairs. After a few seconds, Cyril joined them as well.

Cassia rubbed her eyes, bloodshot from late nights and anxiety. Romy thought she'd aged decades in two days. "I know this will come as a shock, but there needs to be a High Council meeting tonight, and I need you to preside."

"Come again?" She couldn't have heard that correctly. No way in this world would Cassia suggest that Romy, with her unactivated powers, supervise the

Preternatural High Council that she wasn't even a member of.

"I have to stay here with Thora, but the findings of Claude's investigation must be disclosed to Asa Rincewind and his pack, Monsignor Marchland, and the other leaders."

Romy slumped against Dane, and he offered a supportive squeeze to her arm. "Can't you FaceTime them? Zoom call or something?"

"Unfortunately, no. This kind of announcement must be face-to-face and in a formal setting. Everyone bears witness to my verdict, which you will read after disclosing the details of the investigation. As the future high priestess, you exist as the mouthpiece of The One and The Only."

"Well, Mom, I appreciate the vote of confidence, but I gotta sit this one out. I'm not ready to lead the council yet." After a hard swallow, she forced a tight grin. "I'll be there to support Grandmother or Aunt Selene or whoever you get to do it."

"This wasn't an invitation, sweetheart." Cyril leaned forward, elbows on his knees. "This is mandatory."

"You said a *favor*," Romy fired at her mother. "Not an order."

Cassia's eyes fluttered in exhaustion. "Andromeda, I really don't have time to do this with you."

"You're the one who said I can't even move a candlestick so why the hell would you want me to lead your stupid council?"

Wide-eyed, Cyril stood and clapped his hands once. "Dane, that's our cue, bud."

As the men withdrew to the kitchen, Romy didn't take her eyes off her mother. Cassia didn't relent in her stare either. Green eyes to green eyes. Same skin. Same hair. Sometimes even the same attitude. But they were not the same in everything. Romy did not want to be bound by the constraints Cassia created. "This is wrong, Mom. And you know it. You could literally get anybody else."

"I don't want anyone else, Andromeda. I want you. As my daughter and my heir, it's my right to appoint you to stand in for me."

"You say it's your right, and I say you're forcing me to do something I don't want to do."

Her mouth curled into a slight sneer that Romy barely noticed. "Sometimes we have to participate in situations we don't want to for reasons we can't understand. I will say this to you once, Andromeda, and that is all. I need you to hear what I say and what I *don't* say."

Romy nodded but remained quiet.

"You must oversee tonight's meeting. I cannot tell you why, but I don't need to be there. You have to trust that I would never put you in harm's way, nor would I give you a task I thought you were incapable of." Cassia paused. "Do you understand?"

She didn't understand, but she did trust her mother. "Mm-hmm."

"Good. Dane will be at your side."

"And you'll be here? With Thora?"

The muscles in Cassia's jaw tightened as she answered, "Yes."

But Romy knew she was lying.

CHAPTER 12

you are mine and i am yours

Romy sat with Bastian in the Dusk Garden for the third time that week. Last time, he'd offered comfort, but this time, it was strength. She didn't want to preside over the High Council meeting, nor did she believe she should have to. There were far better choices for the assignment. If her mother couldn't attend, fine, but Grandmother still went to the meetings, and she'd been high priestess for many years. Aunt Selene might have been passed over when she was younger, but she was leaps and bounds more qualified to supervise than Romy. Hell, anyone in attendance who'd been to more than one council meeting could lead and probably command more respect. Beyond that, how was Romy supposed to concentrate on Claude Rincewind's death when her baby sister could be dying too?

After Cassia had told Romy the news, she'd rattled on about the sacred role of the high priestess. How she functions as an agent for The One and The Only. Then she'd spouted some bullshit spiel about how duty came before emotions and the coven came before all.

Fuck. That.

Nothing came before Thora. Absolutely nothing.

So why was she here now, with the entire left portion of her body pressed against Bastian's right side, preparing to walk the path to *Tuiteam feòil is fuil?* Peer pressure? The fear of disappointing her parents and the coven? Fear of disappointing herself? Or perhaps because deep within, she *did* care about what had happened with Claude Rincewind, if only for his nephew.

Though she wasn't cold, Romy shivered and inhaled deeply. Sensing her apprehension, Bastian squeezed her hand seven times. She didn't question what the significance of seven was. As it had been from the beginning of their evanescent interactions, Romy simply knew his soul as if she'd resided within him or him inside her. As if those seven words had knitted them together in a past life.

You are mine, and I am yours.

The breadth of the statement didn't scare her. Nor did Bastian make her afraid. But she was a witch, and he was a vampire. Whatever was between them was an impossible dream.

You are mine, and I am yours.

How was this happening? To meet someone and realize an inexplicable connection? The odd twist was that while she experienced complete peace with Bastian, the insatiable hunger she'd felt for Silvan had only increased. When she was with Bastian, she didn't want to indulge in her Silvan fantasies, but being with one man made being with the other all the more appealing. Which was just great because vampires and lycans were mortal enemies. Every stitch of her behavior was prohibited. Forbidden. *Wrong.*

Do you always do everything your mother tells you?

Silvan's question might as well have been a dare because any interaction with the two men and Romy was *on fire*—a desirable, powerful goddess who did exactly as she pleased and abandoned the need to fit in.

Presently, though, her emotions needed to shift to the back burner. She'd need every ounce of fortitude to muddle through this meeting.

Bastian stood, his way of saying it was time. With no instruction, Romy closed her eyes, knowing that when she opened them, she'd be at the entrance of *Tuiteam feòil is fuil* alone.

. . .

Romy led the Delacroixs through the fiery circle and into the ruins, thankful for less pomp and circumstance than her first High Council meeting. The blaze had a green hue, which Romy thought was odd, but it was only her second council meeting. How was she to know if the lights changed colors? Or what they meant?

The moment she took Cassia's seat, she felt the weighted stares of the other preternaturals. Had it not been for the Rincewind Pack's elevated whoops and jeers dominating the scene, she would have heard their whispers too. The moment Asa realized Romy was standing in as high priestess, an ominous silence fell over the crowd.

And then she heard them all.

Where the fuck is Cassia?

Is this some kind of a sick test? A joke?

It's a little girl pretending to be the high priestess.

She can't even do magic yet.

Impostor.

Pretender.

Wannabe witch.

"Everybody *shuttt the fuckkk uppp*!" Silvan shouted in a voice so loud the ground seemed to shake. "Fucking A, you degenerates. Don't want to be here anymore than you do, but the quicker we let the little princess talk, the quicker we get their information on Claude. And then we can get the fuck outta here, aye?"

The pack sounded their rough agreement.

Asa silently fumed at their center.

Romy exhaled a shaky breath, grateful for the intervention. Silvan probably did want to get on with the meeting for the sake of his uncle, but he'd also called her a princess again. Briefly, they locked eyes, and she caught the hint of a smirk.

"Ma'am..." Asa pushed past Silvan with a low snarl. "Forgive my son for his outburst. May I ask where the high priestess is tonight?"

"It's..." Romy cleared her throat. She looked around for something to steady her, but there wasn't anything. There wasn't any*one*. "It's okay. And umm... well..." She froze, unsure of how to begin. Why the hell had her mom done this to her? Did Cassia *want* her to make a fool of herself for some reason?

"Umm... well...?" Asa repeated. He paced in the center of the ruins, more animal than man, and the entire pack, sans Silvan, swayed with his movements.

"Well, she's not coming. I'll be reading the investigation findings and her verdict tonight." Romy prepared for impact.

"Bullshit!" a pack member yelled.

"The high priestess doesn't give a fuck. I told you

this would happen," said another. "It's what we get for leaving *our* business to witches!"

Asa raised a hand above his head. "No. No. I'm certain the high priestess has sat out the meeting because she's caring for your little sister, right?" He didn't give Romy a chance to answer. "Because we can understand that, can't we, Rincewinds? A mother looking after her gravely ill child?"

"We're leaving!" This time, the voice came from the leader of the dwarves, his arms tightly folded over his chest.

"Us too!" a faerie said.

"Friends, please..." Asa exposed his wrists and opened his arm wide as if he were a politician skilled in persuasion. From her vantage point, Romy saw Silvan sneer at the sight and wondered if the two men had as tenuous of a relationship as she did with her mother. "Let's respect Miss Delacroix. After all, if The One and The Only allow, she will be our next high priestess."

The group slowly settled. Asa turned his attention back to Romy. "Miss Delacroix, please tell us what evidence was found regarding my uncle's death."

"We have to wait on Monsignor Marchland," Romy mumbled.

"What about the marshlands?" He tilted his head, confused.

"Marchland! She said *Marchland*!" A wolf-man

howled in rabid delight. “Because his dirty vamps are guilty as shit. Fucking called it!”

“Nooooo, noooo!” Romy’s head shook so fast it made her dizzy. She braced against the podium. No way would she allow anyone to believe her kindhearted Bastian had anything to do with Claude’s death. “I *said*... we have to wait for *Monsignor* Marchland. As is the law.”

The pack riled themselves into another fevered storm, but soon, the fires of *Tuiteam feòil is fuil* dimmed, and the crowd was silent once again. Bastian glided through the ruins and stopped in front of Romy. A low growl rumbled throughout the circle as the Rincewind Pack gathered around Asa.

“Late again, vamp.” Silvan took a step closer, even with Bastian. Romy’s breath hitched. How could two men be so beautiful, so sexy, and so absolutely perfect? Maybe even perfect for her.

Bastian ignored Silvan’s comment and met Romy’s eyes for the first time since the last council meeting. They were crystalline, like the color of the icebergs in Sermilik Fjord off the coast of Greenland. And they pierced Romy down to her core.

“Miss Delacroix, please forgive the delay.” Today’s interpreter was a male faerie. “I’ll take my seat so we can begin.”

“Thank you, Monsignor.”

"Nice of you to make an appearance at your own trial." Silvan's exaggerated eye roll almost made Romy laugh, but she thought better of it when some of the other preternaturals joined in. This wasn't a simple turf war. This was genuine hatred.

"Good for nothin' vamps," a female elf shouted.

A centaur beat the center of his chest and reared up on his hind legs. "They take from us all with no accountability. What does your mother have to say about that, Miss *Delacroix*?"

"Everybody... please... hush." Romy finally found her voice, and surprisingly, the group listened. Braver now, she turned to Asa. "I'm sorry, but the rules say three to seven members. Please send some out."

"Your mother never enforced that rule," Silvan huffed.

"Yes, she did," Romy said boldly. "At the last meeting."

Asa nodded solemnly. "As you wish, ma'am." With a single click of his tongue, he directed the majority of the pack to leave. Silvan crossed his arms and rolled his head back, groaning. She tried not to take it personally, but she knew she'd be thinking about it all night. About *him* all night.

When they were gone, Romy stood.

At the podium, she located the envelope with the verdict inside. Cassia had given specific instructions for her not to read it beforehand. Romy thought that was dumb. Shouldn't she be somewhat prepared for the reactions, which were sure to piss off everyone regardless? Based on the evidence she'd heard, Bastian probably wasn't guilty, but the murderer was likely one of his vampires. What she hoped the envelope contained was an extension to continue searching. Even the idea of declaring Bastian guilty, directly or by association, made her knees weak enough to wobble.

Romy looked over her shoulder. The entire Delacroix family—sans her mother and father—gave a collective nod, endorsing her ephemeral authority. Her grandmother. Selene. Loren. Countless cousins. Great-aunts and uncles. Each of them provided their undivided support. And for the first time in her life, she could actually see herself following in Cassia's footsteps. Maybe she'd do better at the job than she'd thought.

After locating Dane with his lopsided grin, aptly placed in her father's vacant seat, she signaled to her aunt.

"Thank you for coming today," Romy began. "I'll turn this over to Aunt Selene since she's compiled all the evidence."

"You're doing great," Selene whispered as they passed. After setting a binder down, she opened the first page. "Hello, everyone. I echo what our future high priestess said. We do thank all of you for coming on such short notice, but I think we agree that discovering how the Rincewinds were robbed of their beloved family member is vital. My evidence was compiled with the assistance of Dr. Hiller, as well as an investigator from the Fontenot Coven in Shreveport."

A stack of folders levitated from the podium, then floated into the hands of the individual leaders. "Enclosed within this report, you'll find the autopsy of Mr. Rincewind. Forgive me, Asa, I know it's difficult for the family to see these gruesome pictures."

Asa bowed his head and steadied himself on Silvan's shoulder. "Yes'm, it is. Thank you for your sympathy."

"We determined the victim did have marks consistent with a vampire attack. Two puncture wounds spaced half an inch apart. His blood had been drained from his body, and his heart removed."

Red-faced, Silvan jerked the report from his father, read it, then tossed the papers to the ground. Deep, damning lines cut through his brow. More than anything, Romy wished she could be close to him and offer some form of comfort.

"With the help of our friends in the Fontenot Coven..." Selene continued. "We discovered tracks leading from the northeastern area of the Lycan Woods all the way to the Bayou Segnette. From there, the trail leads into Lake Cataouatche, and we surmise the perpetrator followed the water all the way to the Mississippi."

Romy drew back. She'd never heard any of that before.

"Our high priestess herself met with Monsignor Marchland, confirming the whereabouts of his guests, and both of them have been thoroughly vetted and *cleared* by the Preternatural Constibulitaries."

Several groans echoed throughout the council. Selene tapped the podium and brought them to order. "It was the recommendation of the PC to our high priestess that we continue this investigation beginning in Lake Cataouatche and follow the lead to the river. I'll now turn this over to my niece once again as she reads the sacred words of our high priestess. May I remind each of you that her word is law because she is the mouthpiece of The One and The Only."

As Romy traded places with Selene, the older woman leaned in. "I just know Cassia wrote to continue this investigation. It's smooth sailing from here, sweetheart. You've got this."

"Thanks." Romy swallowed the lump in her throat. Despite the earlier triumph, her fear of public speaking had returned tenfold, and she didn't know where to start. Behind her, she could sense Dane's calm and steady resolve. To her right, Silvan... so powerful, so fiery. And on her left, Bastian, with his depth and tenderness.

All three men were so different, and judging from

the icy stares bouncing between the lycan and vampire, none of them would ever get along.

Still, Romy gathered strength from them all.

She tore into the envelope quickly and instead of reading it to herself first, she began reading aloud.

Big. Mistake.

"Regarding the matter of Claude Rincewind's demise, the judgment of Cassiopeia Delacroix is that his death be ruled accidental, and all investigations cease and desist under penalty of imprisonment."

Though Romy could hear herself speaking, she didn't register her words until the first stone ruin crashed at her feet, and a rock hit her in the shoulder. Plumes of powdery dust rose high as the pack collectively shifted, then barked a sound Romy could only describe as a battle cry. Fifty-plus wolves returned to the circle, wrecking everything in their path. Asa and Silvan attempted to regulate them, but the fires, now an iridescent chartreuse, raged out of control, fueled by the crowd's delirium. Disoriented by the smoke, a large centaur stumbled into the podium, smashing it to pieces. Romy jumped out of the way, but her foot caught on a root, and she twisted her ankle.

"Oww... fuckkk. Damn." Her cries alerted four nearby wolves. Drunk off the chaos, they circled her. Stalked her. Her eyes darted from side to side to find a path of escape, but she was trapped. No one could see her in the fiery mess, and it was unlikely anyone could hear her scream either.

With her gaze fixed on the gray wolf she knew would attack, she dug in the dirt and found a piece of the podium slightly bigger than her hand. If she was gonna die, she'd go down fighting. Two wolves charged. The brown one that reached her first pinned her to the ground just as Romy slammed her weapon into the side of his head. The impact knocked him out, but the other wolf locked his jaw onto her empty hand and jerked hard. His bite should have severed several fingers, but when she turned to see the damage, another wolf, a familiar silver one, had pinned the other to the ground. Long, sharp teeth sank into his neck, accompanied by a low growl.

Silvan.

"Don't kill him," she pleaded. "Something's wrong. Look around."

Silvan's amber eyes narrowed as if he thought she was crazy, but he complied, finally seeing what Romy did—a green haze drifting over the entire area. He released his hold but snarled a warning, and the wolf ran off with his tail between his legs.

Silvan nudged Romy's bloody fingers and whimpered.

"I'm okay. I really am."

Unsatisfied, Silvan sniffed twice, and then... he licked her entire hand.

Romy didn't know whether to be mortified or turned on. Was he going to eat her? Was he upset she'd gotten hurt? She didn't speak wolf, and before then, she'd never wanted to.

When he finished, her hand was clean and much less painful. Did he have some sort of healing ability?

"Thank you, Silvan." With his help, she sat up and buried her face into his fur. Romy inhaled, simultaneously calmed and intoxicated by his scent. Pine. Leather. Like the woods in wintertime.

As she gained her bearings, she realized why the other two wolves had never reached her. Bastian stood between them with outstretched arms, emitting some kind of force field. Briefly, he turned and regarded Romy with a look that had the hair on Silvan's back standing in a tall wave, but before the wolf could act, thunder boomed overhead.

From the sound of it, Romy knew it was no ordinary stormcloud... Her grandmother had released her fury upon *Tuiteam feòil is fuil.* But why now? Why, after the lycans and centaurs had destroyed their circle and several preternaturals—including herself—had gotten hurt?

Soft sprinkles quickly turned into a deluge, tamping down the madness and the strange green fire. As the smoke settled, Romy saw Dane first, then Daphne, Selene, and Loren.

Another loud clap of thunder and both the lycan and vampire were gone. It was just as well. Her family didn't need to know everything.

"Romy... oh darling, you're safe." Daphne reached her first and pulled her close. "Forgive me, dear. I'm so sorry this happened. We couldn't move."

"Like... in shock?" Romy asked.

"No!" Loren shook her head. "Like literally paralyzed."

"Was I the only one who noticed a green glow when we first walked in?" Selene collected a broken torch from the muddy ground. "Emotions were high tonight, but this meeting descended into bedlam quickly."

"Was the meeting sabotaged?" Dane's hand went to his mouth as soon as he realized he'd spoken out of turn. "I'm sorry. I didn't mean to insinuate that any of the council leaders would... you know... try to hurt anybody."

"That's exactly what's happened, Dane." Despite no one around them, Daphne's voice lowered an octave. "And you know what that means?"

Romy feared her answer, and by the faces of her family, they did too.

"We have a traitor in our midst."

CHAPTER 13

a path of destruction or a road to life

Finally back at Delacroix Manor, Romy bypassed her parents and ran upstairs to Thora's room. Daphne had escorted her home and reassured her no one could have done anything different to prevent the evening's events. *Unprecedented* was the word she'd used. Truthfully, Romy didn't care if the meeting's mayhem was an everyday occurrence. What mattered to her was that her parents put her in a situation she wasn't prepared for, and then—to add insult to injury—they were sitting on the couch watching the news like nothing was wrong. They weren't even with Thora.

"Sometimes our parents suck, Thor." She smoothed an errant curl from her sister's face. Still unconscious, Thora resembled a sleeping porcelain doll. A single line of fluids ran from a hanging bag to a vein in her forearm, but there were no medications. Romy didn't understand it. Why would they not exhaust every resource, go down every avenue, do *every single thing* in this world to save their daughter?

The opposite of love is not hate. It is indifference. Elie Wiesel's wise words haunted her heart. Didn't they love Thora? Didn't they love *her*?

"Of course, we love you, my little sunrise." Cyril stood in the hallway outside the bedroom as if he was afraid to enter.

"Get out of my head, Dad." Romy was grateful her ability to block had strengthened over the years. Otherwise, Cyril would have had some extremely salacious thoughts to sort through about a lycan and a vampire.

"When you're tired and upset... it's glaringly obvious. You're a neon sign flashing high in the sky like the bat signal." He gestured above them and made a funny face, making it hard for Romy not to snicker. "Can I come in so we can talk?"

Romy shrugged. She really didn't want to debate the same issue again, but he'd always been a persistent man. "Free country."

Cyril went over to Thora and pushed the same wayward curl from the girl's face. "I know you don't understand anything happening with our family right now. Honestly, I'm confused, and so is your mother. It's not easy having kids, Ro. Whether you believe me or not, having you and Thora out in the world is like having my heart exposed twenty-four seven."

"Then why aren't you doing more for her? Why isn't she in a hospital with more medicines instead of this little line of fluid? Why did Mom send me into a fucking gladiator arena with no preparation whatsoever? See my dilemma?"

"I do. And you have every right to be upset about Thora. But we're doing everything we can for her right now. Our laws say we are forbidden from doing anything but believing in her healing and waiting on a miracle, but I promise you, we *are* doing more."

"Tell me, then. What are you doing?"

He shook his head. "I... can't. I just need you to trust me."

"Hmmph. Last time Mom said trust her, I almost got crushed by a centaur. Not giving me much hope here, Dad."

"Your mother would kill me if I told you..."

"So how about trusting *me*? You want me to trust you? Trust me."

Cyril slumped his shoulders as if the weight of the world had descended on them. "Cassia and I went searching for a plant... flower, actually. We know its properties could heal Thora, and we've been combing the swamps, the marshlands, the Lycan Woods, *everywhere* to locate the damn thing."

Romy brightened. Could they be looking for Fenrir's Rose too? "What's the name of the flower?"

"I don't know. Cassia isn't sure. The name was never mentioned."

"Tell me everything." Romy faced him, ready to soak up each detail of his story.

Before he began, Cyril pointed his finger at the door, and it quietly shut. "So your mother has a memory—a faint memory—from when she was younger of her great-grandmother Evadne telling her about how she used this delicate flower with bright-orange blossoms to heal your grandmother when she was a baby. I know you've heard stories about how Iris nearly died giving birth to Daphne and then about her miraculous healing by The One and The Only, but what no one told you is that your grandmother almost died too. And no one told you because no one knew except Evadne and Cassia."

"Where did she find the flower?" If the lycan had lied to her and going to that island was a way to get her alone, she'd be so fucking pissed.

"That's still the great mystery," he said. "Cassia doesn't know."

"And no one else was present when Daphne was born?" Romy wondered. Seemed odd to have only one person present for any birth, especially the birth of a future high priestess.

"No. Evadne had the gift of foresight and knew Iris would have a difficult delivery, so she took them deep into the Lycan Woods, where she delivered your grandmother and saved them both."

She chuckled at the irony. "So what you're saying is that *my* grandmother, who's always adhered to the survival of the fittest teachings of The One and The Only, would have died if *her* grandmother hadn't intervened..."

"Right. And..." he pressed. "Go on..."

Romy thought for a moment, not quite understanding what Cyril wanted her to notice until she considered an important detail about Evadne. With the gift of foresight, she could visualize the future. Did she see Thora's illness over a century ago? Did she tell only one person—Cassia—so she'd know how to save Thora one day? "Okay... I see where you're going. She told Mom so Mom could help Thora."

"And now I'm telling you."

Romy didn't respond to his statement, but it seemed more layered than simply disclosing the information to earn her trust. Cyril needed her to know this story. Maybe he wanted her to find Fenrir's Rose? As she looked out the window onto Napoleon Avenue, movement in the shadow of the streetlight caught her eye. A wolf. *Silvan*. This man would lead her down a path of destruction or a road to life.

Either way, Romy would follow.

CHAPTER 14

calm down, take my hand, follow me, and trust in the unknown

After the pandemonium at the council meeting, Silvan wasn't sure Romy would come at all. By now, her coven would be secreting her away to some clandestine location to be debriefed and sequestered until the danger was properly assessed. Because if anyone was more dramatic than wolves, it was witches.

But the truth was, the night had gotten under his skin, too. He had no idea what had caused half the preternaturals to turn feral and the other half to freeze in place. It had to be supernatural, which meant *someone* there had done it intentionally. To distract. To drive fear. Whatever their motivation, it meant they all had bigger problems than just solving a murder.

Silvan was desperate to shift, but he didn't want to

scare Romy after the pack had nearly mauled her. She'd been genuinely shaken by what had happened, and if not for his quick reaction, she might not even be alive.

And that fucking vamp Bastian. He'd interceded, too, but Silvan wasn't ready to give him a medal. Silvan had no love for Cassia Delacroix, but her dismissal of the investigation was out of character, even for her. Something bigger was happening, and the entire council could implode if they didn't get to the bottom of it soon.

Which, he realized with a derisive snort, might not be the worst thing after all.

The moon was high and nearly full. It called to him like a high-powered magnet, and the need to shift and run—just *run* and run and run—was almost stronger than his raw desire for the crimson witch.

She's not coming. She's seen what your people can do. She's seen how dangerous you are.

It was an utterly insane idea, anyway. The pack had moved Fenrir's Rose to Mar Island—not only because they didn't want witches and faeries stuffing it in their little herb satchels but also because it was dangerous. The guardians of the plant were winged insects whose sting could paralyze and even kill the plant's predators. More than a few of the pack and other preternaturals had lost their lives while attempting to procure the flower. Years before Silvan was born, they'd carefully uprooted and replanted every last rose on the island. Once every five or ten years, someone from the pack ventured over in heavy protective gear to harvest enough for the pack's general use.

"Silvan?"

Silvan nearly leaped out of his skin. He turned, hiding the way she'd unsettled him with just the brush of his name across her lips.

"Almost gave up on ya," he said and started toward her. As he drew near, he could see the wildness hadn't yet died from her searching gaze. "You sure this is what you want to do?"

"Can I... can we... before we start..." Romy sighed with her whole body. Her eyes closed, and they were full of tears when they opened. "Thank you for what you did back there for me. For helping. You saved my life."

Silvan tensed. Sparring was easy. Whatever *this* was... that was another thing entirely. "Shit was bad enough without us murdering the high priestess's daughter."

"You saved my life, and I owe you one." Her head was bowed, her hands folded over her torso. "Whatever you ask of me, I'll do it. Anything."

Silvan's mouth curved into a hungered sneer. "You don't even know what you just said, Romy. If you did, you might take it back."

Romy whipped her head up and looked into his eyes. She was the same little witch as before, but somehow more. Brighter. *Darker.* "I know what I said, Silvan."

His mouth dried up in an instant. So did whatever had promoted him to goad her down a path he never expected her to take. "Mar Island. It's dangerous. There are these insects—"

"I don't care if it's dangerous, and I don't care if it's off-limits. I don't care what it does to me. What... what you do to me." She stepped closer. Her hands, balled into fists, shook at her sides. "If Thora dies, I may as well die with her."

Silvan nodded to himself. He peered into the forest, scratching the back of his neck with a frown. "The boat ride will take about an hour."

"An *hour*?" She gaped at him. "Where the fuck is this island?"

His mouth twisted in amusement. "You have such a foul mouth, Andromeda."

She folded her arms over her chest with a smirk. "I'll show you a foul mouth, Silvan."

Ah, how I wish you would, little witch. "Lake Salvador isn't any deeper than I am tall. It's swampland, princess, and we have a skiff, not an airboat. And the island is on the other end of the lake."

"Can't we drive?"

"Sure, but it would take twice as long, and we'd still need to take a boat at the end."

"Is this some kind of a trap?"

"If I wanted to trap you, I already have you alone." Silvan grinned. "We can test that if you want. Go on. Try to run."

Romy scowled. "You're an asshole."

"A proud one," Silvan replied. "But an asshole who's forgoing sleep to help *your* ass out, so can we get on with it, princess?"

Her whole face flushed. "You don't have to give up sleep for me."

"It's been a long day," Silvan said. He wagged a hand at her, urging her to take it. "Can we skip the part where you act like you *don't* want to spend the next few hours in the swamp with me?"

"I never said—"

"And no games?"

"I'm not playing games!"

"Then calm down, take my hand, follow me, and trust in the unknown."

Romy's lip curled into what seemed like her take on snarling, but it was ridiculously adorable instead. He bit back a laugh and waited.

"I may not have manifested my magic yet, Silvan

Rincewind, but I do have twelve years of tae kwon do, and I'm *fast.*"

"Fair enough, princess." He wagged his hand again, and this time, she took it.

THEY DIDN'T SPEAK AT ALL ON THE LONG WALK to the lake. She seemed to be taking his lead on everything, not just the path. If he looked around, she looked around. If he paused, she paused.

Will you be so obedient when I tie you to my headboard?

"Are we almost there?" she asked, sounding almost timid. His cock turned to hard steel as he imagined directing her to get on her hands and knees and face away; he'd make her wait before approaching slowly, a low growl pressed against her dripping pussy announcing his intention. He'd lave his tongue through her moisture and then bury it in her ass, where it would stay until he'd made her come; just a preview of what she could expect when he spread her cheeks wide and sheathed his cock all the way to the hilt. *Gonna fuck your ass until we both black out, princess.*

All the while, that bastard Marchland watched from the shadows, one hand traveling the length of his own cock in slow approval.

Fuck. No, fuck no.

"Yeah." Silvan cleared the clog from his chest. He adjusted his trousers when she looked away. "Just down here."

He jogged to put distance between them before she read his thoughts in his face—or in his mind. He wouldn't put anything past witches, even the one who'd started to grow on him.

From behind, Romy started laughing maniacally. "Tell me that's *not* the boat."

"Huh?" Silvan turned back, then toward the half-rotted dock. Tied to a piling was his great-grandfather's tin rowboat. It was small, sure, but they didn't build things the way they used to, did they? The thing was solid and unbreakable. It had successfully made hundreds, if not thousands, of trips across Lake Salvador, most of those specifically to harvest Fenrir's Rose. "It might not be a yacht, princess, but it won't flip unless you start dancing."

"Of course I won't be dancing, you jerk," Romy grumbled and stormed down the slight embankment. She jumped onto the dock like she hoped to wake the dead and marched straight to the boat, hands practically glued to her hips.

The lake was dark, with a blanket of foreboding made no better by the smattering of torches from the bayou homes. Next to the dock was an old boathouse. It was little more than a shack but a decent shelter during a downpour.

Silvan pulled up behind her. She leaped in surprise. "Jumpy tonight," he said and stepped into the boat. One foot on a bench, he reached a hand to her. "Come on."

"I can do it," she barked, but her face told another story.

She seemed stubborn enough to draw it out until Labor Day, so he decided on another course. While she was frowning, angling her body in different ways, Silvan launched up, grabbed her around the waist—earning him some delicious squeals he would come like a madman to later—and set her down in the boat.

"You're... you shouldn't touch me unless I ask for it."

Silvan grinned as he unwound the rope from the piling. "Planning to ask me later, then?"

"What? No!" Romy exclaimed, but he heard the truth between her words.

"Sure." Silvan finished and moved to the stern, leaning in to push off from the dock. Once they were in motion, he grabbed both oars, settled in, and nodded for her to sit across from him. "Never been in a rowboat?"

Romy bowed over her knees and shook her head.

"Lake is quiet," he said. "Can you smell that?"

"What?"

"The bayou. It smells different to everyone."

Romy smirked. "A wolf would know."

"Ha." Silvan scoffed. "Wolves have keener senses, true, but humans and preternaturals alike have talked about what the bayou smells like to them. It's always different."

Romy narrowed one eye. "You bring a lot of faeries and elves out here?"

Silvan grinned. "Not too many." *More like none.*

Romy rolled her eyes and cast her gaze into the darkness. "Sweet moss."

"Huh?"

"Smells like sweet moss to me," she said. "Like lilies are growing out of the mossy logs."

"Hm." Silvan nodded to himself. "Smells like a tableau of shit to me. Like seventeen thousand layers of it."

Her eyes flew wide, then her mouth. She started laughing. "You're like, a poet or something, eh?"

Silvan buried a smile downward. "Or something."

"So what... what do you think happened back there? At the meeting?"

Silvan tensed. "Dunno."

"Probably shouldn't tell you this, but my grandmother suggested a traitor. Whoever was behind it got just what they wanted too. Total chaos. It *was* weird. Has anything like it ever happened before?"

"No." He went silent. He didn't know what had happened and wasn't sure he wanted to. But one thing was certain: there *was* a traitor somewhere in the council, and nothing would be the same until they rooted them out.

"I don't think... Silvan, I really don't believe my mom wrote those words." She scrunched her face, shaking her head. "I mean, *yes,* it was her handwriting, but she takes her role very seriously. She wants to find Claude's killer, I promise you. I don't believe for a moment she's given up like that."

"Aye, well, we shouldn't be talking about this. Me and you." He tapped his chest and pointed at her. "Bad enough I'm taking you to a place forbidden to all except us. And that's..." *Haunted.*

Romy brightened in amusement. "Are you... Silvan, are you *scared*?"

"What? No. Fuck no."

Her mouth gaped wide. "You *are*! The big bad wolf is quaking in his boots right now."

"You're out of your mind, princess. I'm not scared of shit. But that island has some dark things. Things you and I aren't prepared for."

"Like the stinging insects?" Her grin broadened.

"You're not taking this seriously."

"I am." She sucked in her bottom lip. "Promise." Her amusement faded to a dark look, and she turned to stare into the bayou. “I have to because my sister could die if we can’t find what I need. So you could tell me a zombie would kill us the second we step foot on that island, and even that wouldn’t be enough to keep me away.”

CHAPTER 15

stick with me and there's no telling what we'll get up to

The moon shone above them in a cloudless sky, guiding their way to Mar Island. Romy trailed her fingers in the water but jerked them onto the side of the boat when Silvan clicked his tongue.

"Wouldn't do that if I were you, princess. You might lose a hand."

She scrunched her nose. "Is the water poisonous like those *scary* insects?" Romy couldn't resist another jab.

"Gators. Haven't you ever been out fishin' at night?" He studied her as though he saw more than her appearance. "Never mind. I forgot I was talking to Delacroix royalty."

"Am not," she huffed, even though his observation was accurate. Her name and station in life had afforded her luxuries but had also put her at a disadvantage. She knew nothing of life outside the coven, outside the safe bubble her parents had created to protect her. "Aren't you supposed to be in wolf form right now?"

Silvan made a sour face, then snickered, appearing like a man and a little boy at the same time.

"I mean, it's nearly full. The moon." She gestured above them. "Isn't that werewolf rule number one?"

"You read too much. In stories and myths, sure, but in real life, no." He rested the paddles in the water, and they nearly stopped. "Am I the first lycan you've ever been alone with?"

"Yep." The question made Romy self-conscious, and she didn't like it. This man, this *wolf* coerced her body to feel things. Unclean, provocative things like him between her legs with two fingers in her pussy and one in her ass. And his mouth... oh fuck... his mouth. That was *exactly* what she wanted to do, fuck his mouth. To stand in this boat and strip, then have his tongue trail a path from the nape of her neck all the way down.

Dammit... *now* she was wet. If Silvan's statement evoked a primal reaction, she couldn't imagine what his touch would do.

"Well, what do you think?" Silvan's smirk told her he was already aware of exactly where her mind had wandered. "Do you like it?" He paused, amber eyes bright with desire. "Or are you scared?"

"Do I have a reason to be?" Boldly, Romy leaned

forward to take the paddles, close enough to feel his hot breath on her neck. Gods, she hungered for him. For his touch, his tongue. Her gaze lingered on the bulge between his legs, less than a foot away from her mouth. How easy would it be to drop to her knees and release the beast from its constraints? Romy would take every delicious inch of him down her throat. She'd squeeze his ass and rake her nails across the tender skin, and when he'd reached the edge, she'd spread her legs wide and receive him deep within her core.

Romy met his eyes, and fire spread through her veins. Silvan, her lycan. He wanted her as much as she wanted him. This man would breathe life into these fantasies and *more* if only she could say the word.

He inched closer. Closer. Closer. She could almost taste him. She *wanted* to taste him.

A night bird called above them, and when Romy jerked away, all the insecurities she fought so hard to repress flooded her mind. What would Silvan want with her when he could have literally any woman in the world? How could she compare to the gorgeous, lithe women of the Rincewind Pack? Big tits. Tiny waists. Long legs. Damn near exotic beauties. Romy had hips and thighs and a mess of unruly red hair. She'd never been with anyone, and until bearing witness to Silvan's cock in all its glory, she'd never even seen a naked man. Romy had no clue how to give a blow job, and he'd been with plenty of women who'd put her to shame. Her lack of experience would be laughable to a man like him.

With one quick move, she took the paddles and slid them back into the water. "I'll row for a while."

"Thanks."

For a moment, they were quiet. Romy focused on the rhythmic trill of cicadas in the cypress trees and took in the beauty around her. Had this not been a mission to help Thora, it might have been a nice first date.

"So does that mean you like being alone with me?" he blurted.

Could Silvan read her thoughts or sense her arousal? Or both? "Why do you care?"

"Why do you always answer a question with a question?"

"Maybe because I don't get you, Silvan Rincewind," she fired back with more irritation than she intended. "Clearly, we're flirting, and we've been doing it for a while. But at the council meeting, you had girls hanging off your arms, and I'm sure crawling out of your bed the following morning. So are you flirting with me for the fun of it or because I'm just another conquest?"

His mouth twisted into a frown. "Neither. I mean, it *is* fun, but you're not a conquest, Romy."

"What am I then?" Why did she ask that? Why did she want to be *anything* to this shifter? Maybe her attraction was a form of rebellion against the life her family expected her to lead. If casual interaction was prohibited, sex was downright taboo, and everyone wanted what they couldn't have, right? "Uggg… forget I asked. Sorry."

"Okay."

Silvan didn't persist, and she liked that about him. Hell, she liked everything about the man. Dammit. Why was he so fucking irresistible? And why did he make her forget her responsibilities so easily? Romy had to get her thoughts back on track. Thora's life depended on it. "So Fenrir's Rose. What do you know about it?"

"My mom did a lot of healing for our pack," he said, a hint of sadness in his tone. "Once, when I was little—just a pup—my brothers and I were out playing near a pond. I was walking across a log and, for some reason, got spooked and fell in the water. A gator, at least an eight-footer, snatched me by my back right paw and started his death roll. I was so scared. I hardly felt a thing, but I could tell without looking that it was bad. My brothers sounded the alarm and half the pack stormed the pond and ripped that gator to shreds. When my father found me, I was delirious and nearly dead."

"Oh, Sil… and your mom…" She led, eager for him to continue.

"Mama worked on me through the night and late into the next day. I know Fenrir's Rose helped, but I swear, she really brought me back with sheer fucking determination. She... was... stubborn." His voice cracked, and Romy swore she saw him wipe his eyes. "Nobody tells you how bad you're gonna miss someone when they're gone. Nobody talks about how the grief sits with you every single fucking day."

How could Romy respond to such a heartfelt disclosure? Silvan had shown her a tender piece of his heart, and he deserved a response, but again, her lack of experience magnified her inadequacies. She'd lost elderly family members and known acquaintances who'd passed, but everyone she cared about was still alive. How could she acknowledge his pain in a way that wouldn't make her seem insensitive? She had no words of wisdom. No motivational mantras. All she had was compassion for his loss.

Maybe that was enough. Maybe sitting there, bearing witness to his grief, was exactly what he needed.

"I'm sorry she's gone," Romy whispered. "I can tell you loved her."

"I did." Silvan cleared his throat and then amended his statement. "I *do*. Always will. Guess that's one of the reasons I want to help you, Romy. To honor my mama. And so you don't have to know..." He didn't finish the sentence.

As Romy opened her mouth to respond, she rowed a stroke, and the paddle hit the bottom of the lake. By her estimation, they seemed to be at least fifty yards away from the island, so she was surprised when Silvan jumped into the water and picked up a tattered rope attached to the bow.

"I'll pull us the rest of the way."

"Clearly. Are you always so impulsive?"

Silvan flashed a devious smile, one that sent an ache directly between Romy's legs. "This is nothin', princess. Stick with me, and there's no telling what we'll get into."

SILVAN TIED THE BOAT TO THE REMNANTS OF A once-functioning dock. Then he dug in his bag and tossed Romy a small amber-colored bottle, which she caught with a startled look.

"Behind both ears, on your forearms and shins," he commanded.

"What's this?"

"Bug spray."

Romy sniffed the contents inside. The scent was strong, oakmoss with a touch of peppermint, and the texture was slightly thicker than water. How in the world could the diluted substance protect them from anything as dangerous as he'd described? Skeptical, she followed his directions but couldn't hide her curiosity. "So if these insects are as bad as you say, shouldn't we have more than watered-down essential oil?"

“Some protective gear might be stashed nearby, but I’m not sure.”

“Are you kidding? There *might* be protective gear?” she repeated. “You didn’t think to get gear from home?”

“Nope.” Silvan emphasized the P with a popping sound. “Couldn’t exactly waltz in and ask for two sets of equipment without telling them I was betraying our laws, now, could I?”

“I’m sorry. I know you’re risking a lot to help me out, and I appreciate it.” The seriousness of this mission had always been apparent to Romy because Thora’s life depended on it. But could Silvan lose his position within his pack too?

“Don’t apologize. If I didn’t want to be out here, I wouldn’t.” Another Cheshire cat smile. “Besides, I wouldn’t pass up the chance to snag another favor from you. Remember?” His hand extended, and Romy accepted. The instant they made contact, a bolt of electricity—a literal current with violet sparks—united them.

She nearly pulled from his grasp until she sensed his peace… and something more. His power. His strength. The wolf’s wild ferocity. While she’d never experienced the electrical surge in her life, she had felt a similar connection before… to Silvan’s sworn enemy. *Bastian*.

“Is… umm… *this* normal?” His free hand went

between them and inside the current still blazing, still linking them. "Feel it, Romy. It's like a cold flame."

Marveling at what they'd created, she touched the tip of a mauve-colored spark. He was right—it was ice and fire at the same time. "Not normal, for sure. It's weird because we touched last night in the woods. Wonder why it didn't happen then?"

"Maybe 'cause you realized I'm not the Big Bad Wolf. Not all the time, at least."

"I'm not afraid of you, Silvan. I trust you." Romy surprised herself with how much she meant that. She did trust him with her life. With Thora's life. "Come on. Let's start looking for this flower."

Mar Island was larger than she'd expected, and its topography was diverse and difficult. Traditionally, South Louisiana was primarily marshland —flat and miry—and while the island had no shortage of swamps, the terrain also had gullies and a lush green forest. It was almost like someone had planted Mississippi's Loess Hill region in the middle of Lake Salvador.

The longer they wandered the shoreline, the more Silvan's face scrunched in confusion. Several times, Romy had heard him mutter how different the land appeared as a child versus an adult. He didn't seem rattled but rather perturbed with himself for not paying better attention to his surroundings.

They searched for an entire hour before eventually returning to the boat.

Silvan stretched his arms behind him and pointed his face at the sky with a defeated groan. "I know it's here, Romy. I know it. We'd stash that extra gear in that hollow cypress, and the rose was about a fourth of a mile to the left, next to a run-off."

"Don't beat yourself up. You were a kid when you came out here last. Sometimes important details don't seem worth committing to memory until you want to remember them." Silvan didn't seem too encouraged, so she squeezed his hand and continued. "I couldn't tell you where we went on vacation when I was twelve if that helps any."

He brightened. "Yeah, princess. It does."

"So what are these baddies called? Do they have a proper name, or are they just *insects*?"

"We've always called them the branka. Magnificent Protector."

"Norse?" she asked. "And a female name?"

"That's right." He pursed his mouth and nodded. "I'm impressed."

"So the lycans think women are stinging winged creatures?"

Silvan closed the gap between them. He bent, even

with her ear, and whispered, "Maybe we think women are badass, fierce guardians who can hold their own."

"I..." She was lightheaded. Inebriated by his scent, his body, the entirety of him. "... like that explanation... very much." Out of the corner of her eye, she saw something she'd missed before. Something she was sure he hadn't noticed either. "Hmm... weird."

Romy released him, but their current lingered. Not as strong yet still a significant charge. She crouched next to a stream. "This isn't stagnant. It's moving."

Their eyes tracked the water upward.

"What if we follow this? Maybe this plant decided it needs fresh water to grow instead of nasty sludge?"

Silvan laughed. "You're a genius."

"Nah. I'm just perfectly ordinary Romy Delacroix. Not even a real witch yet." She cringed. Why would she call attention to her insecurity? Silvan already affected her in ways she couldn't explain. She didn't need him to feel sorry for her too.

He stepped even with her, then brushed his fingers over her cheek. She was on fire again. This man could make her forget everything. "Romy, ordinary is a word I would never use to describe you. Now, come on. Let's find this flower."

. . .

WINDED AFTER THEIR TREK UP THE HILL, THEY took a moment to catch their breaths, bowing with their hands on their knees. Romy stretched back up and surveyed the area, and Silvan did the same.

In perfect concert, they both gasped.

The life-giving orange rose grew in abundance along the banks of the stream. She nearly broke out in a sprint toward the flower, but slowed her eagerness and deferred to him to assess the danger. "Can I?"

"No. Do you see them?"

"See what?"

"The branka?" He pointed at the base of a tree about thirty yards away.

Romy squinted until she saw movement. Brown on brown, the outline of a winged insect half a foot in diameter crawled up the trunk and into the leaves. For a brief second, she saw its color change to green. "Fuck. They're camouflaged." She turned a circle in slow, controlled movements, realizing they were surrounded. The closest one, a juvenile by virtue of his size, flew onto a rock in the water. The bugs resembled wasps, but in addition to their stinger, roughly the size of a full-grown snake fang, they possessed a horn like a rhinoceros beetle.

"Let me go first." His tone was firm, protective. "When we get to the water, get as many flowers as possible, but put them all in your bag. *Slowly*. Like painfully slow, Romy. If you think you're being slow enough, go slower. No sudden movements. No sound. I'll have your back, okay?"

"Mm-hmm," she whispered as she opened her cross-body purse and put on a pair of gloves.

"We should be fine. Their purpose is to guard, not to hurt. They only attack when provoked."

"Provoking them is not in my plan, believe me."

With careful precision, Silvan guided them to the highest concentration of Fenrir's Rose, next to a rock formation with a constant water flow.

Romy was pretty sure St. Charles Parish had no known springs, so it was an odd sight. Silvan seemed equally baffled. After removing the scissors, she made quick work of snipping several plants. When she was up to ten, she leaned into him, revealing the contents of her bag. He held up all the fingers on one hand. Five more to go.

Four.

Three.

On the second to last one, a branka landed square on the one she'd snipped. His body dwarfed the petal underneath, but his shade still changed into a burnt sienna. Silvan glanced over his shoulder and mouthed, "Put it down slowly," which she did. Carefully. So carefully. Confident the branka were undisturbed, they backed away and breathed easier as they started back down the hill.

"Good job, Romy. You did grea—" He stumbled on a loose rock, landing on his knees. "Fuck." Silvan cursed the new rip in his jeans.

"Are you okay?" The flashlight shone on his leg, revealing a tiny cut not much bigger than a scratch. "I have a Band-Aid."

"Nah, it's fine. More pissed about my jeans than anything."

She giggled and ran the tattered fabric through her fingers. "Oh, these jeans that already have ten thousand holes in them?"

"Yep," he joined in. "Except the other holes are *intentional*."

"Ohhhh, intentional holes. My bad."

As they resumed their return journey, Silvan stopped them and turned an ear to the sky. "Do you hear that?"

"No? What am I listening for?"

"Buzzing."

"Buzzing?" she echoed, closing her eyes to concentrate. Finally, she heard what he did, a high-pitched hum that rapidly escalated into a sizzling roar.

"Romy." He cupped the sides of her face, his eyes solemn and full of fear. "Run."

Simultaneously, they realized it would be easier to

slide down the hill, but when they hit the bottom, they took off in a sprint.

"Fuck. Dammit. Shit." Silvan grunted, then yelled, "Head for the woods, and don't look behind you. Find some moss. They hate it."

She didn't have to look. They'd already caught up with them. To her left, she could see a branka the size of a housecat descend onto Silvan's shoulders, but right before its stinger stabbed him, he flipped it onto its back and pierced it with a knife he pulled from his boot.

Romy located a sprawling live oak and hid beneath the tangled moss draping from its branches. She waved to show Silvan the way and didn't breathe again until he was safely sheltered with her.

She wasn't sure how long they waited, but it was long enough to slip a Band-Aid on his minuscule cut.

"I guess my blood drew them," he mused.

"A drop? Little more than a pinprick."

"Hey, great white sharks can detect a drop of blood miles away." The remainder of the branka flew over them, oblivious to their location.

"That's a myth, Jacques Cousteau," she quipped. "It's more like one drop *half* a mile away."

"Still better than me. Wolves can scent a large amount of blood for miles, but it has to be substantial." Silvan stashed a handful of moss down his boots until they overflowed, then he passed some to Romy. "Start stuffing, princess."

"What happened to the branka only attacking when provoked?"

He took in a deep breath and released a heavy sigh. "Hell if I know. It's almost like they've mutated. Still look the same but *definitely* are not the same, ya know? They've changed."

Her mind drifted to a similar conversation she'd heard recently. Not entirely parallel but close enough that she could recall the corresponding words. Altered. Changed. Dr. Bryant had said Thora's metabolic composition was altered. She'd completely changed.

"You ready?" he asked.

"Yeah. What's the plan?"

"I say we keep going farther into the woods. Give them all a chance to get back to their little spring, then we circle back around."

She took his hand, and the purple spark surged. "Lead the way."

CHAPTER 16

all over me

They'd walked half a mile when they came to a clearing roughly the size of several high school football fields. Again, Romy marveled at the size of an island that grew spontaneously like the kudzu snaking along the forest floor.

Silvan surveyed the area with a wary air about him. His behavior fascinated her—a man relying so devotedly on his animal instincts. A man who *was* an animal.

After sniffing the air, Silvan knelt and pressed his ear to the ground. His finger swirled in the dirt, and he touched it to his tongue. Romy had never wished to be dirt so badly. Even now, even when they were likely in greater danger than she'd ever known.

"I doubt you can see it, but straight ahead, at the

end farthest away from us, there's something just before that tree line. Can't make it out from here, though."

"Should we check it out?" She wanted to go. Couldn't explain why, but now that Silvan had mentioned it, she needed to see what it was.

"Yeah. We'll stay on the edge of these trees. You'll stay close, yeah?"

Without thinking, Romy leaned back into his chest. Her ass hit right below his groin, below his cock, so when she arched her back, she could feel it... pulsing, throbbing. She moved again, slower. Silvan's breath hitched in his throat, and he released a low, guttural growl. Another slight twitch and he guided her hands to the trunk of a pecan tree. This time, he angled himself up and pushed against her so hard that Romy cried out at the sheer force of him.

"Do you trust me?" he whispered against her cheek, teeth grazing her skin. How she longed to be devoured by this man. To be consumed. "Do you trust me, Romy?"

No fear resided in Romy's heart. She was ready for whatever Silvan Rincewind wanted. "Yes," she said on an exhale. As soon as she consented, his hand went between them. She felt the sag of his jeans, and then... gods... then... his cock brushed between her legs. "Oh, Sil..."

Silvan repositioned her legs, moving them closer

together for a tighter fit. His first movement was pure pleasure, and to muffle her moan, Romy bit the arm he'd braced on the tree. By the third thrust, her hand was on her waistband. "Please, Silvan. Please."

"Not for your first time, princess. You deserve more for your first time. Besides, we don't have long enough. Once I get you naked, it's gonna be an all-night thing. Maybe longer."

"I need more of you. I need more. I want *more.*" Romy didn't recognize her own voice. It was hers, but older. Full of lust. Her desperation made her weak and strong at the same time.

"Then I'll give you more."

Before Romy could register what he'd done, her shorts were around her feet, and he'd lifted one of her legs onto a nearby log. After a long pause, he growled against her thigh, and her knees buckled. Silvan rotated, and with his back against the tree, he palmed her ass.

"Relax. I've got you." Carefully, he lowered her into his lap, and as if it was the most natural act in the world, she wrapped her legs around his waist. His cock was back in his jeans, but the fabric didn't hide the rock-hard erection pulsing beneath her ass. "Romy... I'm going to kiss you now."

"Uh-huh..." She couldn't speak. She could barely breathe.

Strong hands traveled from her hips to her shoulders

and gathered in her hair. He gave a soft tug, tilting her neck. Gently, he parted her lips, and in that instant, Romy knew she'd do anything this man asked. He pulled away from her mouth only to kiss her cheek, neck, earlobe. "Romy..." His breath was ragged. "I'm going to kiss your pussy now."

Silvan stood with her in his arms, walking them to a clover patch. As he laid her down, his lips found hers again, then traveled down her body inch by inch. Romy shivered when he kissed each thigh, and she spread her legs wider to offer him better access.

She was wet. So fucking wet.

"You are better than I dreamed, princess. Is all this for me?" A finger dipped between her folds, and she heard him groan. He tasted the wetness from his fingers. "Fuck, you're so good. So... is it? Is this for me?"

Y...yes... yes... Sil," she managed to say through gritted teeth. "It's... all... for you."

He laved her sex with his entire tongue, and her eyes rolled back in her head. Was she falling or flying? Was this a dream or reality? Her hips rose to meet his mouth, then bucked against him, yearning for climax. She begged him to move faster so she could find her release, but he would not relent until he'd had his fill.

Silvan drank from Romy like he was dying of thirst, like he'd wandered the desert for a thousand years. One finger went inside her core, then two. His mouth moved in tandem with his hand, taking her higher and higher and higher. Until she was everywhere and nowhere. Until she was weightless. Amethyst sparks blazed and burned the ground beneath them.

"Come all over my face, princess. I want you all over me." Another swirl over her clit, and Romy did exactly as he asked. She heard him cry out, claiming his own pleasure. Silvan climbed up her body until he was even with her mouth and kissed her long and deep.

Somehow, her sex tasted sweeter than it ever had before.

Romy didn't know how long they lay there, but when she saw the sky change from black to midnight blue, she nudged Silvan's shoulder.

"I know. We need to check out the clearing and get back to the boat." After standing, he pulled her up too, then plucked several pieces of clover from her hair. "Romy, you are... fuck... you taste... fuck... I can't speak." Silvan gave an awkward chuckle. "You've fucked me up, princess."

She kept hold of his hand as they resumed their trek. "But you didn't..."

"Are you kidding? I came so fucking hard, and you didn't even touch me. Jesus." He dropped his head as if he were embarrassed. "It was wonderful."

“But I didn’t even do anything.”

“You don’t have to. You’re it, Romy. Everything about...” Before he could complete his thought, he stopped and narrowed his gaze. They weren’t within a distance that she could make out anything more than shapes, but Romy knew Silvan’s shifter senses were impeccable.

“What is it?”

Silvan took off, Romy in tow, stopping directly at the edge of the tree line. “Those look like... hmmpff... that’s dumb.”

Romy squinted and blinked to focus on four white stone pillars. No. Not just pillars. Even at a distance, she could see the design had a wide base and narrowed upward to a point. Was it a monolith? A monument? Or something more? “Is that an... altar?”

“Oh fuckkkk.” He stepped onto the field.

Another step.

Another.

Just as Romy registered the blood stain on one of the altars, a decomposing hand reached through the ground and seized Silvan’s foot. Long claws extended and sank into his boot. Before she could help, his entire lower half had sunk underground. A deafening roar shook the trees, and hundreds of the same deformed, decaying hands sprouted in the field, giving way to arms, heads, torsos, entire bodies clawing their way through the dirt. They were humanoid, yet inhuman. Dead but alive. Though they seemed unable to walk, Romy found no solace in this when Silvan sank deeper with every passing second.

Despite his large size and strength, Silvan struggled to break free from the creature's grasp. She tugged on his arm, hopeful to help dislodge him, but Silvan released her hand as soon as he budged an inch.

"Go," he pleaded, hoarse and strained.

"No, Sil. I'm not leaving you," she cried, wetness pooling in the corners of her eyes.

"Go, Romy. Run. I'll be fine. Trust me."

Across the field, the creatures stood almost as one unit and launched themselves in their direction. Whatever handicap they'd had corrected itself quickly.

"Romy. *Now.*"

Something about the surety in Silvan's voice and earnestness in his amber eyes compelled Romy to listen and then... run.

Backtracking the way they'd come, she ran faster than she'd ever had in her life. Unlike the branka, who were easy to divert, the zombie-like creatures followed, shrieking and groaning like demonic wraiths. There would be no hiding in the moss to escape this time. Over her shoulder, Silvan, now a silver wolf, galloped past her and veered to the right. He barked twice, signaling for her to follow, but the command made no sense. She could see their boat. Why would they go a different direction from their only chance off this island?

Romy started toward the dock, but Silvan barked again. Finally, she saw what he'd seen before her: hundreds of branka hovered at the water's edge.

She followed Silvan as they weaved between trees, up and down hills, never slowing. Romy wondered why she wasn't exhausted or slowing her pace. Her energy had to be from adrenaline, right? She damn sure hadn't turned into a distance runner overnight.

Ahead, two branka ambushed Silvan. He easily overpowered the insects, but right before he ripped off a stinger, he barked three times, instructing Romy to go left. She didn't question how she understood him; she simply did. To Romy, the wolf was as transparent as the man.

"Fuck." Kudzu was thicker in this part of the forest, and Romy struggled to keep pace. "Dammit." After an unfortunate misstep, she found herself tangled in a vine. Her ankle contorted, and she was on her ass after a loud pop, sliding down into a seemingly endless gully.

Unable to slow her fall, she shielded her face with her hands and continued the descent. The last thing she remembered was the welcome cool of deep water and crystalline eyes shining brighter than the sun.

Then the world went dark.

. . .

"Romy, Romy… wake up… wake up."

Romy knew it was him. *Silvan*. She heard his voice. Felt his arms. She even recognized his scent. But she had absolutely no doubt that Bastian had retrieved her from the water and sheltered her from harm. He'd constructed a ward of sorts to protect her. He'd healed the ankle she'd thought she'd broken during the fall and then waited with her for Silvan to arrive.

Holding her hand in his, he'd never uttered a word. Never tried to communicate telepathically. His presence was enough. It always would be.

And then he was simply *gone*.

Silvan cradled her now, kissing her hairline. "Are you okay?"

"Yeah… a little beat up." She searched for evidence that Bastian was still around, still watching. He would be in the shadows, imperceptible to most preternaturals. But not to Romy. "You made it?"

"Wolves are a hell of a lot more slippery than people. They can weasel their way out of just about anything."

"I'm so glad you're okay, Sil." She winced and rolled her mended ankle. "What *are* those things?"

He grimaced. "I don't know, princess, but when I stepped on that field, I triggered every single fucking one on the island."

"Shit. Any idea how we get out of here?"

"Got one in my head, but you're gonna flip…"

Silvan helped her stand and looked her over. "You sure you're not hurt?"

"Nothing too serious." Thanks to Bastian, her ankle was tender but not the searing pain from before his gentle ministrations. "Now, what's the plan?"

His smile was knife-sharp and devious. Also sexy. Everything about him was sexy, including the fact that he was nude and hard as a rock. "You're gonna blast them to hell, Ro."

"Excuse me? Say that again." He had to be joking.

"I said, my little fire witch, you're gonna blast those things to hell..." He caressed her shoulder and sparks shot from her fingertips.

"I'm not a fire witch," she insisted.

"Tell it to the pretty purple sparks, princess."

"I can't so much as move a pen across the room, Silvan. Tonight's little flares are just smoke and mirror magic—not my candescence." Right? Had to be. Romy wouldn't get her hopes up for something that might or might not happen. Thora was closer to activation than she was.

"Have you *tried*?"

"Well... no."

"Try," he pleaded. "For me?"

Even though it was a stupid idea, the dumbest yet, Romy couldn't refuse him. She groaned and closed her eyes, visualizing an inferno and the diverse colors within.

Orange. Gold. Red. Finally, she isolated the purple spark. A violet flame, burning hotter and brighter than any of the others. This was *her* flame. Her fire.

Could this be real? Had her powers finally materialized?

Despite the predicament with Thora, or perhaps because of it, she'd felt more alive in the past few days than she'd ever felt in her life. Romy assumed Silvan and Bastian had been the catalyst, and maybe they were a part of it, but the more she entertained the possibility of blasting those cursed monsters to hell, the easier it was to manifest the flame.

"Holy shit. Look, Romy! Smoke and mirrors, my ass, girl."

Her eyes opened, fixated on the flare hovering above them. Silvan was right. She'd done it. Romy had finally reached her candescence. Fearful for the moment to pass, she turned to Silvan. "We have to do it right now. I don't know how to control this, but I don't want it going anywhere."

"It's not, princess. This is a part of your gift. But you're right. It's time we get the fuck off this island. Follow the big sexy wolf."

As Silvan shifted, Romy could sense his strength, the brute force, the survival instinct, linking to the fire deep within her. Bastian's power joined them somewhere nearby, somewhere no one could see.

She guessed Silvan would *not* like that part if he knew.

Quicker than anticipated, they scaled the ravine's incline, but she was unprepared for the horde of creatures surrounding them. Silvan wasn't kidding when he said he'd activated the monstrosities. Relying on the reflexes she didn't know she had, heat gathered in her core and spilled out her fingertips. Blasts of purple light disintegrated most of their adversaries into dust, and Silvan finished off the stragglers.

But the creatures—whatever they were—were healing. Their mottled, gray flesh and black blood regenerated as they watched in horror. Confusion pooled in Silvan's wild eyes. He signaled to Romy, changing course, and they dashed for the shore.

When they clambered into the boat, thousands of branka launched an aerial raid, targeting Romy. They seemed to know she posed the greater threat. If simple-minded bugs had enough cognitive function to attack as a unit, how much more could those humanoid monsters accomplish if given a chance?

At the same moment, she received the same message in her mind from both Silvan and Bastian, confirming what she'd already realized. In order to escape, she'd have to conjure an explosion. It was a feat of magic she wasn't prepared to attempt, but they had no idea if these new and improved branka could fly off Mar

Island. Could the monsters swim? She didn't want to find out.

As Romy gathered energy, Silvan jumped onto the back of a creature assaulting the boat. The two of them wrestled back and forth, and when Silvan took a blow to his right back leg—the same leg the gator had bitten when he was a pup—Romy lost concentration and directed all her power toward helping him.

I'm shielding him, Romy. Let go. Let me.

Romy gazed at the chaos all around, yet there was peace. *Bastian.*

He was hidden but near. So near.

On an exhale, she released it all. Her fear. Her strength. Her need to control. The sky around the entire shoreline went up in a magenta blaze.

Romy collapsed from exhaustion.

Silvan jumped to the boat's deck in his wolf form but rose as a man. For the second time today, he cradled Romy in his arms. "You did it."

Drained past her limits, she nodded. "Mm-hmm. *We* did."

"Baby, you were the star of that show. I'm gonna get us out of here, okay?"

Another nod, then she drifted to sleep, and Silvan paddled as quickly as his own exhaustion would allow.

An hour later, Silvan woke her with a kiss. He'd put on a pair of sweatpants he'd brought for the trip but was shirtless, and gods, was he beautiful. "We're back, princess."

Romy stretched and smiled. "Thank you so much... for *everything*. I can't wait to get home to Thora." She gave her bag a pat and quickly realized it was no longer full. She looked inside. "Noooonoooonoooo! Silvan..." Out of twelve roses, only one had withstood the fall into the water and the fight. One single rose. "This isn't enough. Oh, Silvan... we've got to go back." Romy snatched a paddle and tried to push off from the bank.

"Fucking hell."

In her peripheral, about twenty yards away, Romy saw a figure shadowed in the pale light of morning.

Bastian.

He knelt and placed a bundle of flowers on the ground.

Fenrir's Rose.

And then, he was gone.

CHAPTER 17

merry jaunts to the land of death

The adrenaline had worn off.

It was the only way to describe the dramatic shift in Romy from badass witch to the whirling tempest standing before him.

"Romy, where did the roses come from?"

She wouldn't answer. Refusal burned in her eyes, along with something else equally terrifying and erotic. He'd never been so torn between running from a woman and fucking her.

"No goddamn way." Silvan exhaled the sudden steam brewing within. He knew exactly how she'd gotten the roses, and it made perfect sense. The whole night he'd felt... no, *known.*

Fucking.

Vamps.

No. *One* vamp. One meddling, murdering, witch-stalking vamp that was begging for a lesson.

"I don't know... I don't know what... I don't know..." Romy's ire disappeared in an instant, replaced by clacking teeth and a shiver that sent her staggering into a tree. "What's happening to me?"

"It's all right, princess. It's all right." He made his way to her, pushing his own anger aside to see to her needs. "Just breathe."

"I can't breathe! I can't..." She turned her face into the cypress bark and sobbed.

Silvan gathered her into his arms. She was as pliant and limp as a doll, and if he hadn't swept her from her feet, she'd have crumpled onto the knobby roots. "You *can.*" He brushed a kiss along her temple and firmed up his hold. He hadn't tried his mother's trick in years. Would it even work? "Can you see it?"

"See what? I can't see anything! Silvan, I can't even—"

"Close your eyes and look at the sky, princess."

"That doesn't even make sense!"

"Hear my voice, love. Close your eyes and follow it." He planted a hard kiss on her mouth to kill her rebuttal. "Do as I say, Andromeda."

She sucked in her bottom lip and nodded, sobbing against his chest.

Silvan inhaled hard and let his mind travel to where

he needed Romy to follow. It wasn't an actual place yet the realest destination he'd ever traveled to. His mother had taken him there so many times that when she died, he missed it almost as much as he missed her; like leaving a home you could never return to.

"Do you see it?"

Romy shuddered in a breath and nodded. "Stars."

"And sky."

"And clouds."

"What else?"

"Peace."

"Peace," Silvan repeated and kissed her again.

"How... where... I could live here. How do you ever leave?" She stirred against his chest, but her pulse had slowed to normal. Her breathing steadied. "Silvan..."

Holding her limp, trusting body in his arms, Silvan at last understood what his pack mates described as heartbreak. It was unthinkable to feel so unbelievably close to someone and know they could never be yours. Untenable. Even if he gathered her tight and ran and ran until his human legs gave out, there would never be a place where they could be anything but enemies.

"I've never shown anyone else. You won't tell anyone?"

"I'll keep your secret as long as I live if you promise to take me here again."

"Of course, love. Whenever you want." His chest

cracked down the middle and split. What they'd seen on the island… as soon as he told his father, the rest of the story would come to light. Everyone would know Silvan had forsaken his pack for a highborn witch he was forbidden from speaking to outside the council meetings.

The strange night on Mar Island with the redheaded princess who had stolen a part of him would be reduced to a dream and nothing more.

Romy's eyes fluttered open. She locked them onto his, searching for something. Her mouth parted. Chin tilted.

Silvan met her demand with a crushing kiss. She moaned and arched for more, wriggling in his hold to extract her arms and wind them around his neck.

"I want you," she panted into his mouth. The words vibrated from her tongue to his. "I need you."

Silvan's cock strained in his pants. Had he ever wanted *anyone* so badly? It would be so easy to lay her down on the bayou floor, spread her legs, and claim her, giving them both an explosive memory to hold on to when the rest faded. He'd have her walking diagonally for a week, a persistent, aching reminder of how crazed with desire he'd been when he'd fucked her into next year.

So why did he stop?

Why did he gently let her down, set her on her feet, and take a step back?

Why, why, why?

His cock had questions.

His mind—and heart—had no answer.

"Sil?" She gazed at him with her doe eyes, wounded.

"Not like this," he said, voice choked. "You've had a big night. You need your rest."

Her glazed eyes suddenly narrowed. "What are you, my father now?"

"No, Romy, it's just—"

"Don't bother."

She crossed her arms and spun away, moving toward the bag of roses the goddamn vampire had brought, swooping in like a John Hughes hero with his fucking boombox.

When she turned back, she was different. Serious. Like the past few minutes hadn't happened at all. "Will these even help? I need magic to apply them, don't I? Obviously, it only happened because we were running for our lives."

Silvan grimaced and took a step toward her. "Romy, no. You manifested tonight. *You. Manifested. Tonight.* If you hadn't gone to the island, it wouldn't have happened, not tonight. But because it did, you're going to take those roses, and *you're* going to save your sister,

Thora. *You.* There's no reason to ever doubt yourself again, and if you do, it's only the fear talking."

Romy considered this as she eyed the bag. He couldn't read her. He wasn't sure he wanted to. "I don't understand how *you* knew about these and my family didn't. This is right up our alley as witches. Shouldn't we have known?"

Silvan shrugged and contorted his mouth to match. "Witches tend to keep to themselves and their coven buddies. Don't want to taint your sacred bloodlines or whatever."

"But Dane knew."

"Your fuckin' nerd boyfriend?"

"He's not my *boyfriend.*"

He buried a smile at the sight of some of her fire returning. "Of course he's not. Probably read it in a book, like nerds do. It's not that Fenrir's Rose is some mythical plant that only exists in fairy tales. It's that no one knows how to find it. You know, except us."

"How has no one else stumbled upon that island? It's not exactly hidden."

"They have," he said. "But when enough of them don't come home, others start to realize it's probably not the best idea to go on merry jaunts to the land of death." He scratched his head. "And who knows how long those zombie fucks have been there, but they make the branka seem like caterpillars."

Romy nodded to herself, still staring into the bag.

"Look, princess, Thora will be different. I don't know exactly how because it's different for everyone, but you gotta make peace with that. You gotta remember, she'll *live* because of you, and whatever the cost, it's worth paying. Because death is final." *Unless you're a fucking unnatural vamp.*

"I don't care if she turns into a cursed wolf like you, as long as she lives."

Silvan snorted. "Gee. Thanks."

"I didn't mean..."

"Sure you didn't."

Romy closed the bag and returned to him. She gazed up, craned up onto her toes, and kissed him. "I won't forget what you did for me, Sil. You could have died, too."

"Eh." He shrugged through the fierce pounding of his heart, hoping she heard his words, not his truth. "I'm built for danger, princess."

Romy burst out laughing between kisses. "You sound like Chuck Norris or something."

"Chuck Norris jokes were so early aughts, girl."

"Tell yourself that the next time you look in the mirror, wolfie."

"Wolfie." Silvan rolled his eyes, but he was smiling on the inside. "How original."

"Like you're the first man to call a rich girl a princess? Please."

Silvan moved his mouth back to hers with a low growl. "But I *am* the first one to make *this* princess come with my skilled tongue, aren't I?"

Romy scoffed. "Then you wussed out on the rest."

Silvan shook his head with a laugh. "I was *trying* to be a gentleman."

"Oh, is that what wolves are known for? Chivalry? Shall I ask one of the women you always have dangling from your arms?"

He smirked. "Ask them who gave them the best nights of their lives."

"Hmph." Romy's nose flared. She nibbled her lip. "I should go. I don't want Thora to wait a minute longer than she has to."

Silvan cleared his throat and crossed his arms, stepping back. "Right. Want me to escort you back?"

Romy shook her head. "I mean, yes, I would like that, but... if we're seen together."

She didn't have to tell *him* how bad that would be. He nodded.

"Tomorrow..."

"What?"

"If everything with Thora is... better..." Romy fumbled for her words. "Maybe we can... pick up... where we left off?"

Silvan grinned and cocked his head. "Are you asking me if I'll fuck you?" He said it as much to taunt her as the asshole vampire spying on them from the shadows.

"So crude," she accused but was smiling wide.

"That wasn't an answer, princess."

"You know what I want." Romy's smile died. "And if everything goes to plan with Thora, I'll need a release." She clutched the bag to her chest and sighed deeply. "So I expect to see you waiting for me tomorrow. Wolfie."

Silvan laughed. "You can count on it, princess."

He watched her disappear into the forest, then waited. Several long, intentional minutes passed before he said, "You can come out now."

Bastian emerged from wherever the fuck he'd been hiding. He reminded Silvan of a Victorian-era ghost with his perfectly angular, pale as the moon face and his utterly antiquated wardrobe. Someone needed to tell the dumbass frilly cuffs went out with the Confederacy.

"She's too pure for you, Silvan Rincewind."

"Holy shit, your voice." Silvan cackled and slapped his chest. "It's so much deeper than I expected, given all the little fairy-tale bitches you choose to speak for you. I guess your balls dropped before you got turned?"

"You know what I say is true."

"So you think *you,* an undead piece of shit who can't even speak to her directly, are better for her? The fuck?"

"Maybe I am." Bastian shrugged. His face was

placid, which pissed Silvan off more. "Maybe neither of us is. But we are both seized with a call to protect her, are we not?"

"A call to protect her? Can you at least speak like you belong to this fucking century, bro?" Silvan calculated the odds of being able to shift *and* take him down before anyone noticed. If he didn't have more of his moon-faced buddies hiding in the bushes, Silvan might even get away with it.

Oddly, his appetite for murder wasn't in top form, though.

Was it Romy? Was it the way she seemed drawn to the centuries-old fuckface standing before him, acting like they had anything in common except her?

If I kill him, she'll never forgive me.

Still, it might be worth it...

"You do know I can read your mind," Bastian said pleasantly. "I'll cease to do so now, for it is impolite, but I thought you should know for the next time you're in the presence of one of my people."

Silvan snorted. "Stalking is your area of expertise, isn't it?"

"Excuse me?"

"That night in the Quarter when you were following Romy?"

Bastian smiled thinly. "But I was not the only one trailing Andromeda, was I?"

Silvan rolled his eyes and started to pace. The primal agitation had begun, and moving was the only way to slow it. *For Romy.* "Fuck, man, I was just getting a sno-ball, and then I smelled your dead ass. Followed the stench and spotted Romy with her nerd, and lo and behold, there *you* were, slinking into the shadows like you always fucking do."

"That's not what you saw in the alley, though, was it, Silvan?" Bastian's smooth grin was as unnatural as the rest of him. "But we have far bigger conundrums to solve at present than who Andromeda is attracted to."

Silvan turned away. Why was he even talking to the creature? What would his father think if he ever learned that his son and heir had not only feasted on a witch until she came all over his face but also had a mostly civil conversation with their actual mortal enemy?

For that matter, why was *he* not more concerned about it?

Was it the vamp? Was he magicking him in some way, forcing calm upon him?

Nah, too easy. Silvan would know if someone was controlling him. He'd spent his life breaking chains.

"The only problem I have is how I'm gonna get home without someone smelling you all over me," Silvan muttered.

"You saw it, Silvan. You saw it on the island."

Silvan groaned and pointed his face at the sky. Of

course he'd fucking seen it. It was all he could do to keep it out of his mind long enough to help Romy.

Light crunching sounded as Bastian drew nearer. He practically glided along the gloaming. Everything about him was so obnoxious Silvan could hardly stand it. "Somebody, some*thing* is preparing for a sacrifice. I would wager that the blood you saw on that altar belongs to someone you care about a great deal."

"If you fucking *dare* say Claude's name—"

Bastian held up both palms in surrender. "You have already drawn that conclusion on your own, so I don't need to say his name. You know I'm right. That Andromeda, by virtue of who she is, is in danger. She's..." The vampire trailed off and pointed his pained grimace into the brush.

Silvan's neck hair stood at attention. He felt the sensation ripple through him, the thought of Romy on that altar eliciting a fierce wave of protection that almost had him shifting involuntarily. He swished his tongue back and forth in his mouth to save face. "Right, and how do I know that altar isn't *yours,* vamp?"

"You do not," Bastian said. "And I can offer no words to assuage you of your suspicions. Your hatred runs deeper than my skill to persuade. But for Andromeda, I suggest you at least try to trust me. You and I, we may never be friends, but even enemies can benefit from calculated partnerships. I would and will do whatever is necessary to protect her. I believe you would and will too. Am I wrong?"

"Of course you're not fucking wrong, but that doesn't mean you're right about the rest," Silvan gruffed. "Blood-soaked altars are a favorite of *your* kind."

"And is that not, by itself, rousing your suspicion? The convenience of the finding?"

Silvan tipped his chin. "Speak English, asshole."

Bastian folded his hands across his torso with a patient look. "When the conclusion seems obvious, it's prudent to ask yourself why. If I wanted to deflect responsibility—or, as you might say, frame someone—then I would make it appear like someone other than me was the culprit."

"You're saying the vamps are being framed for murder?" Silvan raked his hand over his mouth with a bitter laugh. "Isn't that your favorite thing?"

"It's not my favorite thing, no," Bastian said. "What I saw on the island disturbed me as much as it did you. I'm only suggesting Andromeda is safer with both of us looking out for her."

Silvan blinked slowly. "You think I need your permission to protect her?"

"Only as much as I need yours."

"Toush, asshole."

"It's pronounced *too-shay*, but that's neither here nor there. I can count on you?"

"I'm not doing this for you!" Silvan bounded forward. He felt his shoulders slowly rip. *Not now.* "Let's get that really fucking clear right now, *Bastian.* I would never, and I mean never, take an order from you. And if I see you hanging around the Garden District, brooding about like a Dickensian orphan in need of a second helping, you can fucking bet I won't have the same restraint I do now." With a devious grin, he added, "You can thank her magical pussy for calming me enough not to kill you. Later, asshole."

Silvan shifted and bounded away.

CHAPTER 18

we've got some mysteries to solve

Using a food processor, distilled water, and a touch of olive oil, Romy created a paste from the roses they'd collected. The recipe was from the *Divina Maledictio* and was so easy to make she questioned why it was such a secret. Why would anybody keep medicine from the sick if not to control? Why murder a man like Dr. Clive Rice, who only sought to help all preternaturals? Romy's answer was in the questions. *All* preternaturals. The stark reality was that the coven—her coven—deemed themselves as chosen, superior beings. And her ancestors, specifically her grandmother, Alizon, had generated a totalitarian empire where witches reigned superior and other races were second-class citizens.

Delacroix royalty had always been a running joke

Romy assumed no one took seriously, but they did. When she became high priestess, she would work to change their reputation. Silvan and Bastian would help her.

Dane would too. That was the reason she went to his apartment instead of making the paste at her house. Her parents would freak out over her going to Mar Island with Silvan, but Romy was certain they'd understand that part since they were also looking for Fenrir's Rose. But placing herself in mortal danger? Running for her life and fighting horrifying creatures? Nope. They'd never come to terms with that. Despite the urgency to heal Thora, Romy couldn't get the creatures out of her mind. She didn't believe they were preternatural. Maybe long ago they had been, but they'd certainly been corrupted by a black magic practitioner with the intention to destroy. She wasn't familiar with using blood in spell casting. Hell, she didn't know much about spell casting period, but she was certain blood was primarily used for evil. And those creatures... definitely evil.

The magnitude of all she'd overcome in one night was overwhelming. Had Silvan and Bastian not been there with her, Romy would have died. Had her powers not manifested, they might have all died. The candescence was a miracle, but her gift was a marvel—at least in her eyes. All witches had elemental control but traditionally favored one over the others. Secretly, she'd always hoped hers was fire. Selene had been the last fire witch born into the coven, and when the time was right, Romy looked forward to learning from her aunt.

Romy had told Dane everything, minus the interlude in the clover, but he no doubt suspected it. Despite his position as her Chosen, he didn't seem upset when Romy told him that both a lycan and a vampire had come to her aid. Actually, he was intrigued. He'd leaned in, inquiring about the details of their adventures, paying careful attention when Romy described Silvan's shifting or the way she heard Bastian's voice in her head. If she didn't know better, she would swear the two men turned *him* on.

If so, that was erotic as hell.

"Coast is still clear, Ro." Dane peered in the door of Thora's bedroom. He'd offered to come to Delacroix Manor and be Romy's lookout while she gave the medicine, and though she was thankful for the assistance, she needed moral support even more—a skill Dane had in spades.

"And I'm just supposed to put it under her tongue and on her gums?" This seemed too simple. There had to be a catch. No way a paste made from flowers and oil could heal a dying girl.

"That's what the book said."

Thora didn't stir when Romy applied the medicine. No change in her vitals on the monitor, and no movement except the slow and steady rise and fall of her chest.

"It's not working." Dread gathered in the pit of her stomach. She was nauseous. "Dane... it's not working." Why had Romy believed it would? Why had she wasted her time gallivanting to a stupid island when she could have spent valuable time with Thora?

"Have you put your magic to it yet?"

"I... mean... kinda?" She enunciated each word slowly. "I've tried, but I just can't replicate what happened on the island, can I?"

"Well... sure." He slipped inside Thora's room and shut the door. "We just have to get you in the right frame of mind."

"This is hopeless, Dane." Embarrassed, Romy hung her head. Silvan had assured her that she'd manifested her magic, yet she was still as inept as before her candescence. She never assumed the experience would transform her completely, but having more self-confidence than before the change would have been nice.

"Fire magic is special. Think about it. Fire is the most destructive of all the elements. A fire chemically changes anything it touches, which can be a gift in the right hands. But in the wrong ones..."

"A tragedy," she finished.

"Exactly." Dane stepped closer to Romy, then placed his hands on either side of her face. "But it's more than that, Ro. It's *you*. If you believe in yourself half as much as I believe in you, Thora will be kicking our asses in Monopoly again before the morning. You don't have to channel what's already inside you. All you need to do is find it."

Deep within, Romy sensed the same feeling she'd felt before she and Silvan scaled the ravine, when his and Bastian's power joined with hers. A power that seemed to intensify even more with Dane.

"Your eyes, Romy..." Dane's hand went to her lower back, and he moved them in front of Thora's mirror. Her irises were no longer green but a shimmering amethyst. "Try now."

"I won't hurt... this won't burn her?"

Water pooled in Dane's palm. "Won't let that happen."

Disregarding all the limitations that told her she couldn't heal Thora, Romy climbed on top of the bed and straddled her sister's lower half. Hands on the girl's knees, she closed her eyes and went to the flame, separating her spark. The violet blaze grew quickly—wildfire—and spread over everything. Then she was *inside* her sister's body.

Romy recognized Thora's sickness—a dark orb residing in her stomach that gathered good cells and nutrients for itself and released a poison with each beat of Thora's heart. And there was something else... something that nearly terrified Romy to the point of stopping. Fenrir's Rose.

This disease had been *caused* by Fenrir's Rose.

Before she pulled back from Thora, she considered the creatures on the island—if they'd been corrupted with black magic, then it was possible Thora had been too. Possibly by Fenrir's Rose. The how and why were a mystery, one she'd have to put aside solving for now. The flower had healed before, and there was no reason to believe it couldn't again. She could heal Thora. She *would* heal Thora.

The bed groaned beneath her as it levitated off the ground. Heat radiated from her fingers into Thora, into the disease. She could see evidence of the paste she applied, now in fluid form and boiling from her fire, engulfing the orb. Like a blaze incinerating a forest, one second it was there, the next it was gone.

Romy looked up. In the corner of the room, Dane smiled.

"That was the coolest fucking thing I've ever seen." He helped her off the bed, and when her knees buckled, he carried her to a nearby chair.

"But did it work? Please... this has to work." Romy didn't know who she was praying to. She didn't care. Any god who would listen. Any god who could heal.

"Romy? Is that you?" Thora said, her voice small but resolute. "Romy?"

Forgetting her exhaustion, Romy rushed to Thora's side and gathered the girl in her arms. "Oh gods, Thora... you're awake. You're... alive."

"Ro... I can't... see." Tears pooled in the corners of Thora's eyes and fell onto Romy's shoulder. "I... can't see."

Thora will be different. Silvan had warned her this could happen, that Fenrir's Rose might alter Thora somehow. Whatever the cost, it was worth paying. He was right. If her sister was blind, at least she was alive. "We'll figure it out, sweetheart. I promise you." She glanced over her shoulder. "My parents, Dane. Can you get them?"

"On it."

Moments later, Cassia and Cyril embraced Thora, reassuring her as Romy had that they'd find a solution to her blindness, but no debility could take their joy.

"Aren't you going to tell them you healed her?" Dane whispered.

"No." She shook her head and caught her father's gaze. Cyril suspected something, and if he had questions, it would only be a matter of time before Cassia did too. Romy needed to find those answers. "Not yet. We've got some mysteries to solve first."

. . .

Romy waited as long as she could stand it. She had to see them. Both of them.

First, she went to Bastian in the Dusk Gardens, their gardens. She was certain he'd be there... he was always where she needed him to be. Always. Romy wanted to say so much to him, yet words seemed too fragile to explain what had transpired between them. Palm to palm, lifetimes together flashed before them in the darkness. She saw him as a boy and her as a girl wading along the Orkney coast, curtains of color swaying in the night sky. She saw them atop a limestone cliff in Rocamadour —an elderly couple sojourning to the land of their ancestors. And she saw them in the future, lying together on a bed of stone... but they weren't by themselves. Silvan and Dane flanked their sides. Each one there for Romy—yet it was more. *They* were more. There was lust, but there was love. So much love.

Bastian's fingers squeezed tighter and tighter as if she was the only tether in this world keeping him to the ground. He knew she would go to Silvan after she left him. He knew what they would do, yet he remained. He squeezed her hand seven times.

You are mine, and I am yours.

Romy closed her eyes and exhaled. When she opened them, she'd be at the shack next to the dock where Silvan had tied their boat. Bastian would watch them.

When the sun set behind Lake Salvador's horizon, Romy opened the door to the shack. As it had been with Bastian, she knew Silvan would be there… ready for her. Ready for them. She looked to her left. Bastian nodded, offering Romy the approval she didn't need but desired. He wanted this as much as she did. He wanted her happiness, her ecstasy. He wanted her fantasies fulfilled and her dreams realized. Even if he wasn't the source of it, Bastian wanted her to know this intimacy, and for the first time in her life, Romy knew someone—a man—loved her thoroughly, completely. And she loved him.

"I didn't know if you'd come," Silvan said as she stepped inside. Hundreds of candles blazed before her and gave the room a heavenly glow. "I hoped you would."

Her voice was husky when she spoke her first words. "I had to see you."

"How's Thora?" He took a large step to close the distance between them.

"Blind." She placed her hands on his chest and felt the muscles tense underneath her touch. "But alive."

His lips pursed into a frown. "I'm sorry. There's a chance it could eventually resolve itself. Did you tell your paren—"

Romy's thumb went to his lips, and her head moved back and forth slowly. "I didn't tell them. I will, but not now. We have so much to discuss, but I don't want to talk, Silvan. Do you?"

"No," he exhaled, his breath hot on her neck. "I don't. What do you want to do, Romy?"

"You know."

"Tell me," he persisted. "Tell me what you want me to do to you, Romy Delacroix."

"I want..." She blushed, embarrassed of her desires. No. Romy would not be ashamed. These longings were genuine and valid. Her feelings were real. His race only mattered because other people said it did. "I want you inside me, Silvan."

Silvan stepped even with her and caressed her face, a finger trailing from her mouth. "Are you sure?"

"Completely. I'm scared, Sil. Because I've never done this before, but that doesn't mean I don't want you. So don't stop. Never stop."

Romy watched as he transformed. A mortal man. A carnal wolf. Her man... her wolf. Silvan was hers. And she was his. With skilled hands, he laid her down, careful to kiss each place he uncovered. He tugged at her bra, exposing a nipple, taking it to suckle. Romy moaned from the pleasure that rippled within. Wave after wave, her need built until finally, he lapped at one side and pinched the other in tandem, and she came. His mouth trailed downward to her sex, licking her exactly the way he had on the island, except now there were no inhibitions to hold him back. In error, she'd assumed the first time would be the best time, but the instant he stuck his finger in her mouth and then worked it slowly into her ass, Romy knew she hadn't even begun to indulge in what this man could offer.

With his finger in her ass and his tongue lapping at her pussy, Romy spread her legs wider. "More, Sil. Please, more," she begged. "You. I want you."

Silvan sat up and licked his lips, then wasted no time pressing his rock-hard cock inside her entrance. He moved back and forth on his knees, teasing her with the head.

"Oh fuck... gods, yes, Silvan. Please."

"Let me hear it again, princess. Beg for it, love." Hand on his member, he slid the tip inside and tilted upward. She felt the pressure all the way in her shoulders.

Both hands palmed his chin, and Romy leaned up to kiss him. He tasted like heaven. "Please, Silvan Rincewind, I want you to fuck me slow and hard. Can you handle that?" she dared.

"Fuck, Ro..." His head bent, resting on her breast. "I'll do anything for you."

"Then fuck me. Slow. And hard."

"I want to come inside you. Do you want that?"

"Will you lick me afterward?" Romy didn't recognize herself. These were not her words but the words of someone in control of herself, her sensuality. These were the words of a woman.

"Hell yes... are you on bir—"

"Yes!" she screamed, arching her back so his cock would plunge deeper. "Yes. I'm on birth control. Now, fuck me... please... gods, Sil... please... *fuck me.*"

Silvan didn't respond with words. Instead, he did exactly as she asked and buried his cock deep within her core. Romy's head rolled back, and she saw Bastian at the window. Watching. Touching himself. She didn't have to see it to know his hand was on his cock. He'd climax with them as he saw Silvan filling her with his seed. She'd climax thinking of Bastian watching.

Silvan grunted. He was getting close.

She felt his cock twitch, and when he paused for her to contract, she leaned up to kiss him again. "I want you. All of you."

"Oh, Romy... yes..." He pumped hard and let out a roar, now more animal than man, and exploded deep within her pussy. True to his word, Silvan kissed a trail from her neck all the way down and licked between her legs until she came all over his face.

At the window, Bastian nodded his approval.

Romy tilted her head back and sighed.

She'd never felt more alive.

epilogue: bastian

Bastian had never liked Mar Island. It was more the history of the place than the place itself, which appeared like every other island in the deep swamps of Louisiana.

When one had lived as long as Bastian Marchland, though, matters of necessity had little intersection with matters of desire.

Thus, it did not matter how the island left him cold and unsettled because he needed to be there, so he went.

If either Silvan or Andromeda had seen what he'd seen, they would have returned as well. In the throes of fear, they'd witnessed only the remnants of danger, an undead army sent to dispel by any means necessary. But they'd failed to see what that army was protecting. What was happening in the shadows at the very moment they were running from their lives.

Bastian hadn't always been able to split his consciousness. It was one of the rare ways he could feel pain, for one, but it was also terribly rude. He offered respect to every moment that was his, and it was an affront to his intention to be perpetually present.

Yet, at times, necessary.

Once certain Andromeda was safe in her bed, lost to her dreams, Bastian pulled his own corporeal form from slumber. He preferred the astral realm, not least because it was where he could be with *her* but also because it was safer. A witness did not bear the same risk as a participant. One protected his life, and the other exposed it.

Though how many millennia had he survived, despite the inherent risk to a semi-fragile bloodsucker?

Vampiric bravado, an old love had called it, and he was rather chuffed by the moniker, though that was mostly due to his love of the one who had said it. She never remembered it, though, when he found her later, and he always found her.

The shadowed figures he'd seen in the forest now stood over the altar, confirming his suspicion. The night he'd shepherded Andromeda to safety, Bastian had realized what Silvan and she had not. In their terror, they'd interrupted that morning's sacrifice. They'd been watched, and now whoever was behind the killings would know their faces. Their names. Their secrets.

There was no use toiling over it, though. None of that could be helped. What had been, had been. What would be was still being defined.

The figures wore all black, head to toe. They were almost caricatures of villains, dressed as they must have thought terrible people should dress. Bastian could make out nothing of use about them, but he very much recognized the poor bloke huddled, naked, on the altar.

Fenring, one of the fresh vampires who'd been staying with him. Cassia had been right to scold Bastian for not registering Fen and the others quickly enough, but he'd never entertained the notion any of his vampires, fledgling or ancient, were behind the unfortunate end of Claude Rincewind.

There was no joy in the present validation.

Bastian felt a stab of melancholy at the sight of his brother lying in terror in the last moments of his undead life. He could intervene and wanted to. Fenring was precocious and silly, words no one had used to describe Bastian in a great many years, and the boy had brought fresh life to his estate.

That brazen, foolish wolf, Silvan, would have roared into the tableau, teeth gnashing, blood coursing, and he would have died for his recklessness. The creatures beneath the cloaks could only be preternaturals, but what kind, what strength... ahh, one could only discover *that* when it was too late to turn back.

Bastian accepted, with a sinking heart, his role that night was to bear witness so that others might be saved. *Forgive me, Fenring. There will be vengeance when the time is right.*

The last thing he would do for Fenring was not to turn away when the screaming vampire's heart was carved crudely from his chest. He watched, teeth gritted, hands closing into soft fists, memorizing every horrifying second of Fenring's final moments.

The undead army suddenly swarmed in from the forest from all sides. They streamed past Bastian—not *seeing* him at all, which was odd, very odd—and came to a stop just beyond the altar as though awaiting direction.

Bastian straightened, recovering from the small fright. If they hadn't seen him, there was a reason. A good one. Nothing was incidental about anything happening on Mar Island that night, and he'd be a fool to fall into the trap of believing otherwise.

He'd seen the undead soldiers before, though these were different. How... why? Neither answer was clear, but one thing was certain. Such creatures could not be created except from the desiccation of other creatures. Other *preternaturals.*

Fenring's cries halted. One of the figures raised the

heart, and the others chanted, humming in a language unfamiliar to Bastian.

It was the first time in many, many years he'd seen or heard something for the first time.

His mind whirred and whirred. So much he didn't understand. So much he couldn't explain, and therefore could not calculate the danger.

The danger to Andromeda.

His flaunting danger, charging into a devilish cornucopia of horrors, was the opposite of protecting her. What would happen if he were killed? If he were the one upon that altar?

She'd never be safe again.

I'd never search for her again.

I'd never find her again.

Bastian spent the next few hours in meditative solitude. Patience was not a choice so much as a state of being when he'd lived as long as he had and possessed infinite reserves. He hardly noted the passage of time at all until dawn broke, the figures cleared, and the army slunk back from where they'd come.

He was alone.

Making his way to the altar, the foul stench of dead blood greeted him. It grew more pungent with every step, and he had to bury his face in his sleeve when he neared the carnage.

Fenring's body was gone. All that remained was his

stolen heart and a river of blood, pouring from the stones and sinking into the soft earth of the swampland.

Tomorrow, someone would find the body wherever they'd staged it, with discovery in mind. There'd be more anger, more fear, more accusations.

None of that would lead them to justice.

None of that would lead them to peace.

In his heart, Bastian believed the infighting and declarations of war were the precise goal of whoever was behind the sacrifices.

With this in mind, he decided now was not the time to share his findings with Cassia. Not until he had enough facts to balance out the lack of them.

And also because once she saw the fear in his heart and knew the name of it—*Andromeda, Andromeda, Andromeda*—their treasured friendship would come to a crashing halt.

He needed to see Silvan, so he ventured to the Lycan woods.

also by river chastain

THE COMPLICATED ROMANTIC LIFE OF ROMY DELACROIX

Silvan

Bastian

Dane

For more information, and exciting bonus material, visit www.riverchastain.com

also by sarah m. cradit

KINGDOM OF THE WHITE SEA

Kingdom of the White Sea Trilogy

The Kingless Crown

The Broken Realm

The Hidden Kingdom

The Book of All Things

Blackwood Cycle

The Raven and the Rush

The Poison and the Paladin

Southerlands Cycle

The Sylvan and the Sand

The Flame and the Forsaken

Guardians Cycle

The Altruist and the Assassin

The Belle and the Blackbird

The Virtue and the Vixen

Darkwood Cycle

The Melody and the Master

The Hand and the Heart

The Wolf and the Witchling

Sceptre Cycle

The Claw and the Crowned

The Duke and the Disciple

The Tempest and the Tides

* * *

THE SAGA OF CRIMSON & CLOVER

<u>The House of Crimson and Clover Series</u>

The Storm and the Darkness

Shattered

The Illusions of Eventide

Bound

Midnight Dynasty

Asunder

Empire of Shadows

Myths of Midwinter

The Hinterland Veil

The Secrets Amongst the Cypress

Within the Garden of Twilight

House of Dusk, House of Dawn

Midnight Dynasty Series

A Tempest of Discovery

A Storm of Revelations

A Torrent of Deceit

A Squall of Sedition

A Chaos of Awakening

The Seven Series

Nineteen Seventy

Nineteen Seventy-Two

Nineteen Seventy-Three

Nineteen Seventy-Four

Nineteen Seventy-Five

Nineteen Seventy-Six

Nineteen Eighty

Vampires of the Merovingi Series

The Island

and more

The Dusk Trilogy

St. Charles at Dusk: The Story of Oz and Adrienne

Flourish: The Story of Anne Fontaine

Banshee: The Story of Giselle Deschanel

Crimson & Clover Stories

Available as a single collection, The Shorts

Surrender: The Story of Oz and Ana

Shame: The Story of Jonathan St. Andrews

Fire & Ice: The Story of Remy & Fleur

Dark Blessing: The Landry Triplets

Pandora's Box: The Story of Jasper & Pandora

The Menagerie: Oriana's Den of Iniquities

A Band of Heather: The Story of Colleen and Noah

The Ephemeral: The Story of Autumn & Gabriel

Bayou's Edge: The Landry Triplets

For more information, and exciting bonus material, visit www.sarahmcradit.com

also by elizabeth burgess

The Counterplay Series

Counterplay follows four intertwined South Louisiana families and their struggle for power, love, and revenge.

Your move.

Misdirection

Mishap

Misled

Misfire

Misdeed

Misfortune

Misplaced

Mismove

Missing

Mistrust

Counterplay will be a total of fourteen books. Sign up for Elizabeth Burgess' newsletter to ensure you never miss a release.

Misaligned, a prequel, can be enjoyed at any time in the series.

Join Counterplayers, the official Counterplay Reader Group on Facebook for exclusive news, contests, discussion, and more.

about river

A decade ago, two authors befriended each other and soon realized they had quite a bit in common. Aside from their lifelong passion for New Orleans, they also shared the same twisted imagination and gleeful delight in torturing their characters, and at some point, they realized torture is more fun in pairs. Thus, the Complicated Romantic Life of Romy Delacroix was born.

Sarah M. Cradit is the USA Today and International Bestselling author of over forty epic and contemporary fantasy stories, and the creator of the Kingdom of the White Sea and Saga of Crimson & Clover Universes. She and her husband live in a beautiful corner of SE Pennsylvania with their three tiny benevolent pug dictators.

A nurse by trade, Elizabeth Burgess loves incorporating the medical field in each book she writes. Her favorite characters are always flawed, and if you see her wearing any color besides black, you know she's sick. Thanks to her maternal grandparents, she believes she can do anything if she sets her mind to it.

You can find them always deviously devising new decadent pearl clutchers.

www.riverchastain.com

www.ingramcontent.com/pod-product-compliance
Lightning Source LLC
Chambersburg PA
CBHW020335310726
48979CB00015B/2382/J

* 9 7 8 1 9 5 8 7 4 4 3 8 3 *